THE WORLD ROSE

RICHARD BRITTAIN

ISBN: 150235974X
ISBN-13: 978-1502359742

PROLOGUE

Once upon a time, there was a great forest realm. High on a hill, among the yew trees, stood a castle. Inside it lived a princess whose name was Ella Tundra. Her hair was golden-brown and her eyes were blue like the ocean. Her smile could melt the hearts of knights and her voice was delicate like a leaf in the wind. Tundra was in her name but not her nature, for she was neither cold nor bleak like tundra, but warm and vibrant like a meadow in summer. At twenty-three winters old, she was world-renowned. Word of her loveliness had spread around the globe to distant lands and far-reaching empires.

Ella's dainty feet padded the purple carpet of her bedchamber. She drew open a mauve silk curtain and stepped onto a balcony, to gaze across a plateau of treetops, above which a thin layer of clouds drifted before a crescent moon. The princess leaned over the balustrade and a cool breeze caused her shoulder-length hair to flow back. Hearing a twig snap in the forest below, she peered down there.

Suddenly, a loud and chilling wolf howl coursed through the crisp air of the hilltop, and Ella jumped in shock. Nearly falling off the balcony, she fumbled for the support of the timber railing and grasped it tightly. Her hair was strewn across her face as she retreated into her room and closed the stained glass door.

Ella spun on her toes and her large eyes fell upon a fawn bulldog sitting in a wicker basket. His presence made her feel safe after that fright, and Ella sighed as she placed hands on hips, staring directly at her canine companion. The bulldog avoided eye contact, as he felt a tad unsettled when the pretty princess locked her gaze on him, though he enjoyed the attention. As she drew nearer, his cracked black nose sniffled and his furry form quivered.

"Oh Duncan, when will I meet my one true love? Who holds the key to my heart?" Ella tilted her head, pouting at Duncan, and the bulldog simply pouted back up at her. It was about the only facial expression he was capable of with those prominent, drooping jowls.

The princess let her pet melt for a bit longer before she bent forward to stroke him, rubbing his ears and scratching him with scarlet fingernails. The stout dog inclined his head affectionately as his short tail wagged, his eyes welled up and his tongue slid out. He was just beginning to slump on his cushion when suddenly he

1

lurched up and arched his powerful neck.

Startled by the abrupt change in behaviour, Ella pulled her hand away. Duncan's floppy ears had become rigid and pointed. The flailing tongue that hung out whenever he was relaxed disappeared inside his mouth, his dark lips curled into an oval and a black hole formed between. Fangs emerged and whiskers quivered. The bulldog's whole face contorted into a snarl and his eyes fixated on the other side of the room. Ella's gaze followed Duncan's and she screamed when she saw it too.

A green-and-brown toad hopped across the stone floor just beyond the edge of the carpet. Duncan's body tensed and then he bolted for the rude intruder, who frantically scrambled along, propelled forward by its springy hind legs. As the bulldog bounded, he seemed to jump in slow and exaggerated motions as if to show the terrified toad that he could hop higher. Duncan leapt above his prey and his paws came down to trap the unfortunate amphibian.

But his nails found only the hard surface beneath, and Duncan's face screwed in surprise that the toad had vanished. Ella gasped and rushed to see what was happening. The incensed mutt turned his attention to a crack in the adjacent stone wall, through which the little critter must have escaped. Ella leaned down and also noticed a gap between two blocks, but she remained behind her bulldog's broad shoulders as she was worried that the toad would leap out at any moment. Duncan furiously clawed at the wall, obsessed with catching the slippery scamp and seemingly outraged that it had not accepted its fate as his new toy.

Part of the princess wanted to tell her dog to stop harassing the poor creature, but she was also not keen on the thought of the slimy thing lurking in her room. It was difficult to make Duncan obey her when he got this excited anyway, so Ella just sighed and watched.

Duncan relentlessly scratched away with talon-like claws and a jingling was heard as one block shuddered. After a few more swipes, the grey slab dislodged completely. Duncan appeared thrilled that his tenacious work had borne fruit as the rock slid across the floor. The bulldog lowered his head to look into the wall's new chasm and the princess also peered into the small void. No toad could be seen, but Ella's eyes fell upon a glimmering object partially concealed by moss. "What is that?"

Forgetting about the toad, who must have fled through further cracks, Duncan strained for this new curio. Paws probed for the shiny thing which had aroused the interest of his mistress, but the boisterous bulldog barked in frustration as his efforts came to nothing.

Ella decided to get it herself. However, she did not want to put her hand in there for fear of finding something unpleasant, so she took a shoe from under her bed and placed it in the gap, to scoop the glinting object out. As Ella extracted her blue slipper, the trinket glided out beneath, but before she could grab it, Duncan had pounced and seized it in his mouth. He trotted triumphantly to his basket, tail wagging in delight as the prize clinked against his teeth.

"Oh Duncan, that's metal. Spit it out!" Ella demanded, but the bulldog's face scrunched in stubborn refusal as he attempted to chew on the hard item. "SPIT IT OUT!" Ella put a hand in front of Duncan's jaw while glaring at him. With an expression masked by guilt, he glanced up at the angry princess and opened his mouth. The glistening object slipped off his tongue and dropped onto the red cushion.

Duncan panted loudly after a most exciting situation. In an attempt to heal the rift with his mistress, he playfully raised his paw, which Ella squeezed, while her other hand picked up the trinket. Her brow furrowed as she stared at an elaborate flower-shaped ornament. It was coated in Duncan's saliva, so the princess grabbed a cloth and wiped it clean.

Ella was looking at a red porcelain rose with a spiral of gold twisted around its green stem. She wondered if the beautiful ornament had any meaning as her gaze followed the lustrous yellow metal coiling like a snake. The golden shaft extruded beneath the base of the stem and Ella noticed some jagged teeth running along one side of that extrusion. She realised that she was holding a key, the head of which was the flower and the tip of which was the bottom.

The princess experienced a moment of exhilaration after determining the object's purpose. She squinted and searched for any letters, symbols or words which might yield further clues, but found none. Ella ran her fingers along the smooth surface of the artificial rose and looked at Duncan. "What on earth is this key for?" But the bulldog merely yawned, slumped lazily in his basket with a sullen frown on his face.

Suddenly the door to the bedchamber flung open. A male guard stood in the frame and stammered, "P-Princess, your father... H-he's..."

Ella's eyes widened. She ran past the man, out of her room, and rushed down a spiral staircase so quickly that she almost tumbled. After sprinting across an onyx hall, she pushed open a heavy oaken door.

"Father!" The silver-haired monarch lay on his bed, peaceful, pale and still. The nursemaid by the dead king's side wept quietly while holding his hand. Ella started to sob.

CHAPTER 1 – THE FAIRY QUEEN

The death of the 'Druid King', as they sometimes called him, came as more of a shock than a surprise. The elderly monarch had been confined to his bedchamber with illness for weeks. Ella had been by her father's side for much of that time, but she was full of regret that she was not there at his moment of passing away. It had happened suddenly and without warning, but he at least died a peaceful death.

The princess mourned intensely, and it was two days after the event when she gained sufficient clarity of mind to consider what the situation meant for her. King Aelfwoad, an immensely popular figure who had united the various forest realms, had ruled Celtia for half a century. But now Ella would become queen and her coronation would occur in a matter of days.

The burden of responsibility weighed down on her slender shoulders, but it was a challenge the dainty princess was ready to accept. Her father had been a good teacher, one who educed qualities in people rather than imposed knowledge. Life experience was more valuable than rigid scholarship. To create one's own destiny was more important than learning the works of others.

Hence, Ella had generally been allowed a degree of freedom. Being a princess gave her a life of relative independence and quietness, but now only a few more days of that remained. There were some things that Ella knew she would simply be unable to do once she became the Queen of Celtia. One thing in particular, she had been planning for a while.

Deep in the woods dwelt a great seer who went by the name of Saxophyllus. Ella had always wanted to visit him and hear his profound wisdom for herself, but the establishment neither approved of such 'wizardry' nor trusted the old man. Ella was a good girl with rebellious tendencies and she was determined to see the seer. It seemed prudent to do so before she had the responsibilities of a monarch, and she also felt in need of some final guidance before assuming power. Ella knew it was a difficult day's trek to the seer's abode. As she looked out a window, she decided that there was still enough light to begin her quest now.

Though dainty, Ella was not the excessively sheltered type of princess. She would often go wandering in the forest nearby, occasionally on her own but more usually with her dog. She packed a bag with the basics required for two days and slung it on a sturdy cedar staff. Ella wore a long evergreen dress over her curved body, brown walking boots on her small feet and a dark silk veil to cover her fair hair.

The princess and the bulldog descended the tower's spiral staircase and slipped out of a back door. They entered the woods and immediately set a brisk walking pace. Ella had a rough idea of where she needed to go, knowing what hills to traverse while the position of the sun would inform her of direction. She was unaware of any path which led to the seer's abode but hoped to find one once nearer.

Across a carpet of foliage and fallen branches, Ella journeyed with her stout, stalwart companion. Rays of light shone through gaps in the leaves of trees and the atmosphere was altogether pleasant. Jay-birds hopped elusively from branch to branch while ravens strutted like black squires along the forest floor. Warblers, tits, finches and doves chirped their own unique songs, complementing the steady drill of the woodpecker to form a wondrous symphony of nature.

The pair saw mushrooms of many kinds, buttercups and shaggy parasols, vivid blues and greens, yellow shelves which jutted out of trees and brown fairy rings upon the ground. Some appeared doughy, fresh and edible while others were dark, stagnant and reeked of toxic odour. Butterflies fluttered and dragonflies flickered through the cool afternoon air. Squirrels sprinted up trees, always maintaining a good distance from Duncan, who knew that they were too fast for him anyway.

After half an hour of travelling through such serene woods, the princess and the bulldog descended a slope and came across a sparkling brook. Ella hopped over stepping stones while Duncan trotted straight through and splashed water up to his undercarriage. He paused in the middle of the stream to savour some of the clear, refreshing liquid, his long tongue lapping loudly while Ella sat on a fallen log.

A little way up the stream, beyond the slender valley they were in, Ella noticed a small bridge, which must mean that there was also a trail. "Come on," she said to Duncan, whose thirst had been quenched. Water dripped from his drooping jowls as he cocked his head before bounding excitedly after the princess. They proceeded along a bank of rough grassland and saw a fairly well-beaten trail on either side of the limestone bridge.

Just as they reached it, a bugle-like sound blared from their right. They turned their heads to see a short man blowing what looked like a cattle horn. He wore a loose brown garb with fur boots and his thick blonde hair was combed to one side. After removing the instrument from his lips, the young fellow flashed a toothy smile and strode confidently towards the pair. The princess stared cautiously with big blue eyes while the bulldog seemed alert and ready to pounce.

"Greetings, greetings!" The man nodded twice while grinning like a drunkard, his green eyes somewhat glazed and maniacal.

"Hello," Ella responded simply and continued to study him.

The stranger took a dramatic bow. "I am Gullivander, bard of renown!" He pulled another instrument from his hip, panpipes, and blew into them while prancing from side to side. Ella started to grin in bemusement and Duncan began to bark.

Gullivander chuckled and exclaimed, "This dog knows not fine music when he hears it!" Duncan's tail wagged as he jumped up at the bard, who stumbled a bit before petting the frisky mutt.

Ella smirked. "He doesn't bark like that when I play the flute."

"Oh thou play the flute!" The man's eyes lit up and his lips curled in delight. "Thou must be a bardess!" He stroked the head of the bulldog who was now licking the curious items hanging from the bard's belt.

"I am no bardess," Ella retorted, "but a princess. My name is Ella Tundra." She curved her mouth into a practised slight frown which created a demeanour of haughty disdain.

Gullivander's jaw dropped and the panpipes fell from his hand, striking the earthen trail. The bard stared at the princess in silent awe for a few moments. "Thou art… No, surely thou jest."

Ella pulled down her dark veil which made all of her face and hair visible. The man's green eyes scanned the maiden's golden-brown tresses and eminently elegant features. He let out a little scream of joy. "By the harp of Garrick, you really are the revered princess!"

Gullivander fell to his knees and clasped his hands together as though in prayer. "And I thought the odes to your beauty were but ballads of folklore, songs of myth and legend, yet here I can witness it for my own eyes! It is crystal clear. You are the most splendorous woman I have ever seen." He looked down at Ella's shoes as though unworthy of viewing her royal countenance.

Ella shrugged. "Thanks, but I don't believe that."

Gullivander was so humbled and amazed by the presence of the beautiful princess at the small stone bridge in the midst of the woods. The normally confident bard's lips quivered and he stuttered on his words. "W-What brings your royal loveliness here?"

"I am journeying west to find the seer known as Saxophyllus."

"Saxophyllus," the bard murmured, still on his knees. He looked at the dirt and furrowed his brow. "I can help you!" he said suddenly and raised a finger. "I know where the old man lives!"

Ella smiled. "Any directions would be useful because I am not entirely sure where I am going."

Gullivander paused in thought with a hand on his chin. "It is at least eight hours from here." He glanced up at the sky. "But there are a mere two hours of light remaining in the day."

The princess nodded. "I know. I did not expect to reach him tonight. We will camp out."

The bard suddenly scoffed, his face cloaked in incredulity. "A princess? Camping out? In these woods?" He shook his head vigorously. "*Boulderdash!* I have never heard the like. Why, there is a little tavern but an hour's walk up this trail. It is in the right direction for the wizard too. I can take you there, where you can surely eat and sleep."

Ella tilted her head. "Eh, alright. That does sound quite nice. Thank you."

The bard stood up in a theatrical manner and they followed the trail into a pine forest. "I would let you stay at mine of course, but it is a couple of hours back that way." Gullivander pointed to the other side of the bridge behind.

"I very much appreciate your kindness."

The coniferous woods were particularly tranquil and quite different to the deciduous woods which they had walked through previously. Rather than a layer of leaves, the ground was covered by a carpet of fine green moss which looked lush and comfortable.

As they strolled, the bard had much to inquire of the princess. He had heard legends about the Tundra dynasty and wanted to know which were true, having never met such royalty himself, so Gullivander told tales, sung ballads and recited poems. Ella happily obliged the keen performer, educating him of the deeds of her forebears while dismissing those stories which were works of fiction. One example was a limerick about Ella's great-grandfather, King Wedgewood, founder of the Tundra dynasty.

"Old Duke Wedgewood of Tundra,
He rode into battle like thunder,
But slayed the wrong man,
The chief of his clan,
And so became king by a blunder."

Ella frowned. "No, that's not true. He became king because the ruler and his only heir were killed in battle. But the enemy got them, not Wedgewood or any other member of their clan. My great-grandfather helped win the war and everyone agreed that he ought to become king. If he had slain his own leader, why would they have elected him?"

Gullivander nodded. "Fair enough, your majesty." He asked the princess no further questions for fear of offending her.

The trail twisted around and verged on a low fence surrounding a field. Two donkeys ambled towards the trio, their heads bobbing up and down in turn as they seemed to prance in choreographed manner. The animals stopped at the fence and the humans petted their snouts while Duncan sniffed their hooves.

Ella looked at Gullivander. "Say, you are a bard, so you must be full of lore." She reached into her bag and pulled out the ornamental key that she had found days earlier. "Perhaps you might have some idea of what this key is for."

The bard examined the ornate porcelain rose and the gold metal wrapped around its stem. "I have never seen such a key, your majesty, but it does look quite marvellous. Sorry… Most of my lore pertains to the epic rather than the practical! I would say that the old sage should be able to help though."

"Don't worry. Indeed, I was thinking the same. I shall ask him."

"Where did you find it?"

"At my castle, hidden within a stone wall."

"How intriguing. It sounds like a whole new fairy tale waiting to be written!"

Ella smiled. The sun hugged the horizon and the last rays of daylight stretched through trees just as the trio reached their destination. A small round tower of coarse stone stood by the trail. A wooden placard hung outside *The Roundhouse*, which looked more like a farm granary than a tavern.

Gullivander pulled the striped door open and Ella stepped onto the ceramic floor of a cosy room. The walls were the same stone as the exterior and the low ceiling was wood. There were only three tables, one long and of dark timber, and two round ones of light shades. Various chairs and stools dotted the chamber and a fire burned on the left. Directly opposite the entrance was a collection of barrels and kegs with boards on top of them which constituted the bar area.

In its centre stood a petite young woman with long brown hair parted in the middle. She was less than five feet tall and wore a simple beige dress. The barmaid smiled brightly and held her hands together as she watched the guests enter. As Duncan trotted in behind the two humans, his claws made a much more audible sound against the hard, sandy tiles.

"Sophie!" said Gullivander as he walked towards the little barmaid.

"Greetings Gully."

"Sophie," the bard repeated. "You will not believe who I have here with me!"

Sophie tilted her head and observed the evergreen-clad woman. "Umm…"

"Go on, guess!"

But Ella did not seem to want to be the object of Gully's game, so she walked up to the barmaid and extended her hand. "Nice to meet you, Sophie. I am Ella Tundra."

The short woman gasped and put a hand over her mouth, glancing at the bard and then back to the princess. She was not sure how to act in such a situation, how to greet a personage of such esteem, but she was more down-to-earth than Gully and keen to make the royal maiden feel welcome. Sophie enthusiastically shook Ella's hand, clasping it with both of her own.

"'Tis the greatest of honours, m'lady." The barmaid rushed to a cabinet, bouncing on her feet, and pulled out a bottle. "Our finest wine." She popped it open. "This is on the house, your majesty!"

Ella smiled but shook her head. "Oh, don't be silly. I have money, but thank you." The princess reached into her purse and placed a dozen coins on the table. "May we have dinner here too?"

Sophie poured some deep red wine into a silver chalice, which she handed to Ella. "Of course, your highness!" She poured more wine into a less fancy mug for Gully.

The two said their thanks, picked up their cups and sat at the long table in the middle of the room. Sophie quickly set about multitasking as she began to prepare a three-course meal. Duncan moved to the fireplace and lay on his side at the edge of the hearth to bask in the warm flames.

"Sophie, the damsel has no place to stay tonight," Gullivander mentioned.

"Then she must stay here tonight with us!"

"Are you sure?" Ella asked. "I do not wish to be too much trouble."

"Certainly, your majesty! 'Tis the highest privilege. We have a room upstairs you may take, and your dog is welcome to sleep down here by the fire."

"Thank you very much. That is most lovely of you."

"Not at all. Gully, would you like to lodge too?"

"Oh no, I'm fine. I am performing in the village fayre tomorrow morning, so I must return to my place tonight."

Sophie chopped onions on a wooden board while Ella sipped at her chalice and relaxed in the homely tavern. The red wine had an exquisitely rich, fruity taste and went straight to her head. She murmured in delight and leaned back in her chair, round eyes glinting as she gazed into the fire.

The first course was mushroom soup with hazelnut bread. Ella and Gullivander were both hungry and ate it quickly, expressing their approval of the dish. When the bard finished, he took out his lute and started to strum. He played mellifluous melodies and sung well-known favourites, cheery tunes and wistful ballads. Ella jigged her head to the mellow music, impressed by the breadth of the bard's talents. Then he began to play an airy piece which she had not heard before.

"They call her the Fairy Queen,
For she is delicate as a sprite,
Lucky are those who have seen,
Her warm smile glowing bright,
How seldom has there ever been,
Such a fine and wondrous sight,
And she need not primp or preen,
For she always looks a delight."

The blonde bard's fingers lingered on pensive chords as the melody became slower and deeper.

"To see her luscious hair,
Golden tresses long and fair,
To see her blue eyes keen,
Will keep you from despair,
She wore a dress of evergreen,
For she is like a grove of pine,
A forest eternal and serene,
Oh most lovely Fairy Queen,
If only you could be mine."

Gullivander's eyes locked onto Ella's but she raised her cup to her lips and took a long sip. The main course arrived, a hearty hog and vegetable stew. While the princess and the bard consumed the wholesome fare, Duncan fed on a plentiful supply of scraps. He soon fell asleep and snored loudly by the fireplace, only to be awoken by the bard's resumption of music. The entertainer performed on panpipes, an array of percussion as well as his lute, seeking to dazzle the pretty princess who was of about the same age.

Sophie gave her guests some of the tavern's finest beverages to sample – exotic wine, rich ale and sweet mead – but Ella only had a small taste of each as she did not wish to get drunk. For dessert, a magnificent strawberry tart was laid on the table. Sophie had made it for the fayre the next day but she did not mention that, privately deciding that the princess was worthier of the pudding than the villagers. The little woman cut slices of the large tart and served them in bowls with cream.

Ella picked up her silver spoon and queried, "So how exactly do I get to the seer's home tomorrow?"

Gully nodded as he swallowed a big piece of the delicious dessert. "From here, you must follow the trail for four hours, until a river. Cross over it and walk upstream for a further four hours. At the end of a valley, you'll reach a forest – can't miss it – and in that forest does the old sage dwell." He scooped up another spoonful of tart and cream before adding, "Would you like me to take you there?"

"You have a fayre to perform in tomorrow," Ella said with a grin.

"I would cancel it for you," the bard offered as his youthful green eyes gazed upon the princess.

"I will be fine. Your directions sound easy enough and I have

Duncan for company, but thank you very much."

Gullivander shrugged. He took up his lute and declared that he had one more piece to perform. He strummed a light, fluttering tune and started to sing.

"How shall I call that pretty young dame?
The beautiful maiden who came,
That alluring enchanting flame,
Who plays on my heart like a game,
Yet I cannot give her blame,
For to a girl of such fame,
Are we not all the same?
She is Elegant, Lovely, Luscious, Amazing,
So ELLA must be her name."

There was a pause in the music as Gullivander looked into Ella's eyes. She smiled and then he played a rich and dreamy theme.

"Tundra is her last but she is more like an oasis,
She is the lily of the valley,
She is the rose of the world,
She is my garden of paradise."

The musician finished with a deft flourish of notes. Ella drunk the last contents of her chalice to hide her face and Gully put his lute away before getting up.

Ella also stood up. "Thank you for everything, Gullivander. I really enjoyed the music. I would like to invite you to my coronation in two days. There should be an opportunity for you to play."

The bard gaped at the princess and for the first time had no words. "Wow, I don't know what to say to that. I most gratefully accept your royal loveliness's invitation!"

Ella offered her hand, which Gullivander leaned down and kissed, closing his eyes as he savoured the moment. He said goodbye to Sophie and Duncan before bowing dramatically to the princess, and departed through the striped door.

The silence brought about by the absence of the rambunctious bard was immediately striking. For a while, only the gentle roar of the fire and the snores of Duncan could be heard. But Gullivander's musical notes still seemed to linger in the air, popping in and out of the ether.

Ella's eyes drooped as fatigue overcame her and she asked Sophie to take her to her room. The petite woman led the princess up a narrow staircase and unlocked a cracked wooden door, entering a circular chamber while loose boards creaked beneath. In the middle of the room was a plain double bed with white blankets and a pillow, there was a simple wardrobe to one side and a round window let in some moonlight.

Sophie lit a candle on the bedside table and beamed her smile. "There you go, your highness. If you need anything, I will most likely be asleep in the basement, but I do not mind being woken."

"Thank you again. I will see you in the morning." When Sophie left, Ella collapsed on the bed, drew the linen blankets over her body and quickly fell into a deep sleep. Sophie went down to the main room and cleared everything away while Duncan snoozed on the floor.

Ella dreamed that night. She found herself in a dark corridor. On her right, the wall was made of stone blocks, but on her left it consisted of pure earth. A torch hung nearby but the flame flickered and faded. Ella looked up and saw the roots of plants and trees dangling from a soil ceiling, which meant that she was underground.

Her footsteps echoed as she walked down the corridor. A toneless hum came from the black depths behind, growing gradually louder, so Ella hurried along. On her right, she saw a rusty door with a large bronze lock in its centre. As the eerie drone drew nearer, Ella tugged on the lock, and then remembered that she had a key in her pocket.

She pulled out the rose key, grasped the flower head and plunged the golden tip into the lock. It fit inside but would not turn, so Ella persisted and then it clicked. The key rotated and the lock fell to the ground.

The princess pushed open the door and was immediately overcome by a haze of spiralling mists. Beyond the fog stood a tall figure in a shining suit of armour. Ella ran towards him, but tripped on the root of a tree and fell on her face.

CHAPTER 2 – AN EVERLASTING DYNASTY

Ella jolted in her bed as she awoke. Daylight shone through the window and robins flew around outside. The princess got up, folded the blanket and descended the staircase to the tavern floor, where Duncan was scampering about, but there was no sign of Sophie, so Ella left twelve coins and exited through the striped door.

The princess looked down the trail and saw long grasses swaying in a gentle breeze. The sky was pink as the sun peeked over a distant hilltop and Ella felt jolly now that she was outside. She remembered the instructions given by the bard; four hours down this trail and about the same length of time up a river.

Ella skipped and Duncan trotted in a sprightly manner alongside her. The princess hummed a tune that she had learnt yesterday, a song about the valour of King Herald, her grandfather. The birds chirped their own merry ditties as flashes of green and yellow feathers jumped between trees.

At one point, a line of badgers crossed the track a short distance before the travellers. Duncan was so bemused by the sight of the black-and-white creatures scurrying in single file that, rather than charge, he simply watched while Ella grinned with a hand on her hip. In the first three hours of the morning, the pair made good progress and barely paused, but then they were forced to stop by what lay ahead.

Two huge, horned, brown bovine animals blocked the trail. One stood with its snout pointing up, sniffing the air, while the other lay on its front and chewed grass. Each horn was as long as a human's arm, curved upwards and sharp at the tip. The princess and the bulldog moved tentatively closer, step by step, as they tried to establish whether these beasts, who had barely acknowledged their presence, were even interested in them. Ella suddenly felt a hand on her shoulder and jumped, turning her head.

"Hello there, my love. Do not fear. These cows are perfectly alright. Highland cattle you see. About as docile as they come." The tall man appeared to have horns himself, but that was just his hairstyle. Two dyed purple cones extended from his head and

wobbled as he spoke. "I'm merely resting them. Oxen they aren't."
The stranger chuckled, almost seeming to be talking to himself as he
rarely glanced at the princess.

"They are yours?" Ella looked at the large cows.

"Indeed. I am on my way to Teffyr to sell some wares." The
purple-haired man gestured at some packs on the ground which had
presumably been removed from the backs of the cattle.

"You're a merchant then?" Ella studied the talkative fellow, who
had the lightest sky blue eyes and skin which appeared silvery. He
was thin, at least six feet tall and wore a navy-blue outfit trimmed
with mottled gold edges. A mulberry cape hung over his back.

"I am. My name is Jandrole Heth." He offered a lengthy hand.

"Ella." The maiden daintily shook the merchant's hand.

Jandrole's reaction was nothing other than a polite nod. Either he
did not know of the famous princess or he assumed that this was
another Ella. Perhaps after a day of travel, she did not look quite as
stunning as she often did. Her veil covered her hair and some of her
face, but she was beautiful nonetheless, and he was handsome too if a
little odd-looking. The princess decided not to reveal her regal
identity on this occasion.

"It is rare to see a young maiden walking through the woods alone,
though I see your canine companion. Where are you going, if you
don't mind me asking? Or are you just at a bit of a loose end?"

"No," Ella said curtly to the inquisitive individual. "I am on my
way to meet someone."

"Ah, I see." Jandrole swallowed, seeming suddenly nervous in the
presence of Ella's scrutinizing gaze. "Well, if we are going the same
way, perhaps we could walk together?"

"Very well." Ella offered a smile. "I need to find a river about an
hour down this trail."

"Then let me waste no more of your time." The merchant hoisted
the cargo onto the cows and tied the various bags into place. In the
midst of one of the packs was an elaborate wooden chest with a
gilded lock on its front. After ensuring that the loads were safely
fixed, Jandrole stepped between the cattle and tugged on their reins.

"What do you sell?" asked Ella.

"Oh everything really," replied the merchant in that quick and
eager tone which Ella had already learned was characteristic of him.
"I come from a land very far away. Originally I brought wine, and it

is the finest you will ever taste. But over the past year, I have moved from town to town, realm to realm, trading goods of all and every manner. Spices, jewellery, weapons, crockery… I am even hoping to sell these cows soon."

"That's nice. You must live an interesting life."

"You could say that. I arrived in this particular realm only a few weeks ago. Are you familiar with it?"

"Yes. If there is anything that you would like to know, then ask away, for I have lived here all my life."

The merchant glanced at the canopy of trees above. "What are the taxes like? I haven't had to pay any yet."

"Nothing out of the ordinary," Ella said. "Similar to the taxes in most other realms around here, I suppose."

Jandrole nodded. "Are there any particular dangers that I should be aware of?"

"This is a fairly safe area, but there are bandits operating along the coastal regions. I would avoid heading there, as you could be ambushed. Merchants carrying goods like yourself tend to be their prime targets."

"Ah. Thank you for the information. I usually avoid main roads for that reason. Bandits rarely waylay minor trails like this. They are called 'highwaymen' after all." Jandrole paused. "Oh, there is one thing that interests me especially about this realm. I have heard stories of a beautiful princess who lives high up on a hill. Eleanor, I believe her name is?"

Ella smiled faintly as the dark silk veil hung across her face. "It's Ella actually. I should know, as I was named after her."

"How wonderful! You must be of a similar age too."

"Indeed. I was born a few weeks after the great ceremony which took place following the princess's birth. Ella became a popular name for babies that year, obviously, and my mother chose it for me."

"*Phenomenal!* Aren't we lucky to be living in the realm of such a celebrated figure? Perhaps one day I can entice the fair princess with my wine." Jandrole chuckled. "I must meet her before I die!"

"Sometimes dreams come true. Oh, that must be the river." The sound of flowing water could be heard.

"Ah yes," Jandrole murmured, as they saw a wooden bridge, and crossed it.

Ella turned to her new friend. "Now I must leave you, Jandrole

Heth."

"What a pity, for I have greatly enjoyed your company for the short time that we have been together. It has truly been a pleasure, Ella. When will I see you again?"

The princess shrugged. "Soon, hopefully. I wish you safe journeys." She waved and the purple-haired man bowed before turning. His mulberry cape billowed between the cattle as he trudged along the trail.

The river sparkled in the midday sun and Ella gazed upstream. A thick carpet of long grass verged on the river but a rough trail of flattened shoots made a path discernible. Ella went up the slope followed by Duncan. She was a proficient hiker but he was more likely to encounter difficulties, being a stocky and unathletic breed. The bulldog was soon panting and his lengthy tongue hung out as he struggled to keep up with his mistress.

"Come along now Duncan." Occasionally the bulldog looked like he wanted to stop moving entirely, but Ella had some scraps of dried meat with which to entice him. The princess plucked daisies and dandelions and placed them in her hair. She smiled as the day grew warmer and merrily bounced along, stretching her arms out on either side of her swaying form.

After a short, steep ascent, the pair came to relatively flat ground. The river meandered sharply and they entered a splendid valley. A lilac haze covered the fields on both sides of the river. The travellers were now in open meadowland and the princess frolicked while the bulldog bounded joyfully through the flowers.

The valley seemed to amplify the heat of the sun. A cool breeze offered some relief but bushes and trees high up swayed in a stronger wind which did not reach the pair. Swifts danced through the air in sparse flocks, twisting and turning so sharply that it was impossible to follow any one. A buzzard loomed above and cast its shadow on the field as it circled and squawked.

The lilac haze turned into a crimson sea as the visitors entered a poppy field. At the end of this smaller meadow stood a forest, which must be the one that the bard had mentioned. A sense of euphoria came over the princess as she approached. Upon reaching the edge of the woods, she turned around to look at the stunning landscape which they had walked through. The wind swept through the red and purple fields like a wave through an ocean.

They stepped into the forest and a stark contrast became apparent. The atmosphere was still and deathly quiet. Save for the occasional and distant caw, no creature made a sound in these woods. The stench of stagnant water pervaded the air. Ella and Duncan ambled across knotted roots as the ground became soggy and loose. All around, pools of muck filled craters verged by the knobbly legs of dying trees. Twisted limbs pointed at awkward angles as leafless branches slowly sunk to their demise. This seemed to be more of a swamp than a forest, and it became difficult to navigate the ridges of dry land, particularly for the stout bulldog whose legs were getting soaked.

The deeper they penetrated the strange world, the darker it became. It dawned on Ella that she had no real idea of what she was looking for. Gullivander had simply stated that the seer dwelled in these woods, and hopefully that meant he would be easy to find. But what if the bard was wrong? What if the seer was not home, or what if he no longer lived here? Who on earth *would* live here? Suddenly it struck the princess that this whole journey may have been a ridiculous idea fuelled by naïve optimism.

Then they saw a flash of grey. A gangly heron swooped down and landed on the far side of a pond. The tall bird stood completely motionless and stared into the greenish-grey waters, either not noticing or not caring about the two wanderers who looked so out of place in this territory. The silent heron was hardly a comforting sight, but it was reassuring that something lived in this rotten realm.

Suddenly, a sheet of white lightning illuminated the dreary landscape. For just a second, the travellers could see far through the gaunt woodland. Menacing silhouettes seemed to lurk in the distance only to fade into the darkness. Thunder rumbled in the skies and the heavens opened. What had seemed a wonderful day in the idyllic valley not long ago had turned into something wretched and woeful. Rain pattered onto the canopy which was concealed by a dense layer of tangled vines and branches. At least it provided shelter, as the water only poured into those existing pools.

The princess and the bulldog saw a surprisingly healthy-looking willow tree ahead, a most welcome growth of green among the vast grey bog. They walked towards it and pushed aside a slender curtain of foliage. As they entered the willow enclosure, they found themselves in a beautiful haven. The long leaves provided a serene sanctuary in the midst of the dreadful domain.

Ella looked down at Duncan, who was glancing around fearfully and jumping whenever the thunder struck. The princess sat down against the thick tree trunk and comforted her bulldog, who began to appear a bit more assured.

A sudden breeze made the willow leaves flutter, and then the sound of chimes was heard. It jingled like the disharmonious melody of an ethereal world. Duncan tilted his head to evaluate the delicate tune of assorted metal notes, which seemed to be coming from high on the other side of the tree. Ella wandered around there and saw a ladder of wooden rungs swaying on two long strands of rope.

"Ella Tundra," a croaky voice called.

The princess looked up and saw the outline of a person standing among the branches. "Mister Saxophyllus?"

"That is I. Come up."

Ella glanced at Duncan, who would never make it up the ladder. "What about my dog?"

"Try this." A whirring sound ensued, as a pulley was lowered, consisting of a thick rope with a cloth harness. The princess was uncertain that such a device could support her weighty bulldog, but she tied him in and watched as he rose. Of the many weird and wacky sights that Ella had witnessed, seeing Duncan levitate probably came top. His facial expression was blank and droopy, as though he had just settled in his basket for the night, while his meaty frame swung and his legs dangled freely.

Ella ascended the ladder, remaining alongside her pet in case something went wrong. She passed those metal chimes and eventually reached a wooden platform. A short old man turned a wheel to reel in the pulley mechanism's rope. He had a large head with messy grey hair to his shoulders, a crooked nose, small ochre eyes and prominent brows. A scraggly beard which curled at the ends adorned the corners of his angular face. Barely more than five feet tall, he wore a mud-streaked olive robe. Ella helped Duncan onto the platform and released him from the harness.

"Greetings," said Saxophyllus.

"Hello. How did you know who I was? Were you expecting me?"

"No, I guessed. Come, let us talk inside." The elderly seer led the pair onto a loose bridge over a swamp, but Duncan proceeded hesitantly as he glanced through gaps between planks. From the middle of the bridge, the grey clouds could be seen, and a sudden soaking was enough to prompt the bulldog to quicken his step.

At the end of the bridge was a larger tree which supported a hexagonal house. Saxophyllus opened his front door and an intensely woody smell hit them. The dwelling consisted of a single room built around a broad trunk and an open window provided the only source of light.

"I was just making some tea. Would you like some?" Saxophyllus hobbled to a copper kettle.

"Yes please. That would be lovely."

"Sit down." Saxophyllus gestured to a carved chair in front of a stump table. Ella sat and felt a sense of relief at having finally reached her destination. Even if the seer did not enlighten her with the profound wisdom for which she had come, at least she had found him, and his home was surreally pleasant. Duncan collapsed on the floor and rested his head at Ella's feet. The bulldog's brown eyes studied the interesting old man.

Saxophyllus poured tea into two metal cups and placed them on the table. Ella looked into the clear vermilion liquid, which had an enticing scent like that of wild berries. The skies crackled and rain pounded the roof while water could be heard trickling through pipes along the interior of the treehouse. The seer lit a thick red candle which illuminated the whole room, casting vast shadows on the walls that piqued Duncan's curiosity.

"I am sorry about your father," Saxophyllus said.

Ella nodded. "Thank you. I know you and he did not have the best of relationships, but I believe that you were both wise men."

The seer smiled. "I only ever saw him when he was a prince, at a similar time to you actually, just before his coronation. That was half a century ago, but he did marvellous things in this realm as ruler."

"Well, hopefully it won't be the same with me. I mean, I hope I will get to see you when I am queen."

Saxophyllus chuckled. "I hope so too because I won't be alive in another fifty years. I understand that you are to become the monarch within days?"

"In two days, yes. But I wanted to visit you first, because I know that you are a seer of great insight, and I hope to gain some of your knowledge."

A raven flashed across the window. "Knowledge must never be

forced," said the wizened sage as he raised his teacup to his lips.

Ella smirked. "My father used to say that. See, you are more alike than people would have."

"I will answer any questions you have to the best of my abilities, but first I must know if you would like to have dinner here?"

The candle gave off fumes of an unusual odour, like bitter plums. Ella watched the flickering flame and then looked up at her host. "That would be marvellous, Mister Saxophyllus. Thank you very much."

"Excellent." Saxophyllus rose from his seat to begin the culinary preparations. "You may sleep here too, of course. There is plenty of space."

Ella glanced around the room. "Well, that would be perfect. Duncan and I are both tired."

Saxophyllus rifled through a cluttered cupboard while the princess sipped her tea, which left a sharp aniseed aftertaste. Combined with the strong candle fumes, the berry brew caused Ella to gradually slump in her chair, and she drifted off.

She awoke to the pleasant smell of stew. Steam billowed from a cooking pot gurgling atop a small stove as an aroma of nuts, vegetables and herbs wafted. "It is ready," the seer announced.

"Oh, sorry. I fell asleep." Ella rubbed her neck. "It smells delicious."

Saxophyllus scooped out three portions with a ladle. "It's pea and nut stew with onions and herbs." He brought the bowls to the table. Ella had never heard of such a combination before, but it looked quite appetising. Saxophyllus glanced at Duncan. "I'll give him his when it's cooled a little."

The sky outside was now dark, so the seer walked to the window and closed a shutter before returning to his seat. He stirred the contents of his bowl with a spoon and the princess did the same.

Ella swallowed some warm pea froth and crunched on a hazelnut while thinking about what she would ask the seer. Duncan eagerly lapped up the vegetarian stew despite being more of a meat lover. These were small portions, which explained the man's slight figure, and it was not long before Ella finished hers. When Saxophyllus finished his, he got up and cleared things away while Ella thanked him again.

"Now then," said the seer as he hobbled back to his chair. "Have you decided what you wish to ask me?"

The princess furrowed her brow, appearing deep in thought. "I think so." She reached for her bag, rummaged around inside it and pulled out a rose key. Ella leaned forward to place it on the table when a particularly loud rumble struck, causing her to jolt and drop the key. The red porcelain rose with gold twisted around its stem clattered against the table and rolled towards the seer. Duncan roused and barked at the sounds, pacing in circles before he calmed down.

Saxophyllus picked up the key and examined it while Ella watched him. His forehead creased and he said nothing for a couple of minutes, seeming quite troubled. "Where did you get this key?"

"I found it in a wall within my room, at my castle. A toad led me to it."

Saxophyllus nodded slowly, his expression unflinching as his ochre eyes continued to study the intricate key.

Ella spoke again, "I had just asked about finding my true love when it appeared, too. And I had a dream in which this key led me to a man wearing a shining suit of armour. I have a feeling that it will help me find my one true love."

Saxophyllus pursed his lips. The candle fumes partially concealed his face so that the princess could no longer see his expression.

"A key without a lock is useless," the seer began. "But the one you seek for love possesses also a lock matching this key, and it guards a chest carrying tremendous treasures. For many mighty kings and princes desire you, but one shall rise above the rest. And he brings an everlasting dynasty. He will come to conquer this realm and there will be a great battle. When you know that he is the one, you will collapse in a field of cloth and gold, and he will carry you home."

There was silence for a few moments following the prophecy. Ella was trembling and her lips quivering as she looked at the old man with wide eyes. The storm showed no signs of abating as thunder and lightning continued to strike.

"Th-That can't be right." Ella shook her head. "If someone loved me, why would he fight me?"

"Perhaps you will not know that you love him until you have fought him." The seer paused. "And, when you truly love something, you are prepared to fight for it. And the greater one's fight, the greater one's final reward."

The princess curled her lips in anger. "I am not a reward! And I want love, not treasure or land or a dynasty."

Saxophyllus shrugged. "Well this man appears to have all of those things. You may not love him for them, but he has them nonetheless. And now that you are to become queen, you must think about such things, just as your father did. For what is a monarch without wealth, a realm without land and a throne without a dynasty?"

Ella stared scornfully at the seer, who held his hands up defensively. "I have answered your questions as best I can." The red candle flickered out while Ella sat silently raging. Saxophyllus then said, "You must rest, for you are tired. You have a long journey home tomorrow, and important days beyond it."

Ella began to nod slowly. The seer unfolded a quilted mattress and placed it on the floor for the princess along with a thick blanket. "Thank you," she murmured. Saxophyllus hobbled to a heap of straw on the far side of the room and Ella eventually moved to her bed.

CHAPTER 3 – A MOONLIT KNIGHT

It was midday when Ella awoke in the home of the seer. Even though she had slept through the night and morning, it felt like she had only just gone to bed. Duncan was already awake and sitting on his hind legs as he observed the rising princess. Ella stood up and walked around the tree trunk in the middle of the room to locate the seer.

The front door opened and Saxophyllus entered, carrying a sack, which he dropped to the floor. "Ah, her majesty is up. I was just about to wake you, for it is time to begin your journey home."

Ella looked out at the sky and nodded, having not intended to stay here for this long. She needed to get back to her castle tonight because her coronation was tomorrow. "Indeed." The princess quickly packed her bag.

"I will walk with you to the river crossing, where you can pick up the trail." The seer grabbed a walking stick.

"There is no need," Ella said. "That is four hours away."

"I must go that way anyway."

"Very well. Thank you."

They left the treehouse and crossed the bridge over the swamp. Ella descended the ladder of the willow tree and Duncan was lowered on the pulley. The trio walked through the grey forest in the direction of the brightness on its perimeter.

They were soon in pleasant meadowland and ambled through the fields of crimson and lilac. Ella munched on a fruit, her breakfast, as they skirted the river. Now that they followed the sparkling water downstream, they could advance swiftly.

Saxophyllus, Ella and Duncan reached the bridge in the mid-afternoon. The seer leaned on his staff as he turned to the princess. "You must cross this bridge of wood now, but tomorrow you must cross the bridge of accession." He chuckled. "I wish you luck."

"Thank you. I appreciate everything that you have said and done for me, Saxophyllus." They embraced each other and bade farewell. The seer turned and hobbled west while Ella and Duncan went east.

Return journeys always seemed quicker than outward journeys, and the pair progressed happily along the trail. Both the princess and the bulldog were keen to return to the luxury of their castle and the hours elapsed without incident.

It was early evening when they passed *The Roundhouse*, that quaint stone tavern, but Ella decided not to go inside because time was at a premium. The woods were eerily quiet and the pair had not seen a soul since the seer had left them. It was also cooler than yesterday and the crispness intensified as the sun lowered beyond a peak.

Half an hour after they passed the tavern, the dusk began in earnest, and Ella soon realised that it was more unsettling than expected. The princess had never travelled through the woods at night, and had assumed that it would not be all that different to the day, but it was very different indeed. The darkness shrouded almost everything and each sound became a potential lurking menace. The last chill of the spring became biting and the two could soon see their breaths in front of them.

The sounds of the forest changed as the creatures of the twilight emerged. Ella did not know whether they were birds or animals, but they made the most ghastly sounds; shrill screeches and frenzied titters. Duncan became anxious and trotted along so quickly that he was constantly on the verge of breaking into a run.

They began to hear the swift, soft pattering of a creature's footsteps to their right. It was probably just a fox, perhaps even a new friend, Ella thought optimistically. In a way, it was reassuring that the creature could be heard scuttering, because it made it less of an unknown.

They then heard a similar pattering on the left of the trail, and Ella looked around, but saw nothing. She stopped and the rustling stopped. The princess glanced down at her bulldog, who appeared scared. Ella considered returning to the tavern for the night after all, but it was quite a way back. Her coronation would begin tomorrow afternoon and she would need all morning to get ready, so she could not take chances. The bright full moon offered some encouragement and they pressed on.

But as soon as they continued, the subtle scuttering continued. Ella sighed loudly and told herself that it was probably just a couple of curious creatures who had not seen people on the trail at this hour. The sounds faded before disappearing and Ella grinned down at Duncan. "See? Nothing." The stone bridge could not be too far away, and from there it was only half an hour to the castle.

Suddenly the pattering commenced again on both sides, but now it sounded like three or four animals in total. Ella's smile inverted into a frown as she increased her pace, and Duncan scurried along too while frequently glancing into the dark woods. The princess started to sing, which made her feel more confident and might also have the effect of scaring the creatures away.

Twigs snapped as the minions of the night kept up with the pair's brisk pace. The periods of silence between sounds grew shorter until they were a constant presence. On all sides were the dexterous footsteps of four-legged creatures against the forest floor. Ella and Duncan were now being pursued by several animals.

Duncan started to whimper as he stared into the trees on his right. Ella followed his gaze and then screamed. Two glinting eyes peered from low down through the foliage. Ella looked around to see more sets of eyes glowing in the moonlight on the left, ahead and behind.

The princess panicked and ran. The bulldog hurried along while frantically turning his head from side to side. Branches splintered and leaves flew across the trail as the shadowy stalkers gave chase. Suddenly, one jumped out ahead.

Bold as brass, the grey wolf stood and stared. Ella halted momentarily but then continued running in the hope that it might frighten the animal. He was barely bigger than Duncan, and freezing in place would look like weakness. The predator let them pass but pressed his nose against the side of the scampering bulldog. Duncan reacted by snapping his large jaw and the wolf backed off, but followed, along with those in the woods.

As Ella ran, she saw another wolf bounding through the thickets on her left. The princess screamed and the nimble animal leapt from the verge and sunk his teeth into her boot. Fangs pierced leather but missed Ella's foot by a fraction of an inch as she felt smooth enamel sliding along the edge of her skin. The princess swung her staff at her assailant but he barely flinched. Ella hopped on her free foot as she tried to pull away but the wolf's jaw was clamped on her boot. Two more of the grey stalkers circled around Duncan though his growling kept them at bay.

As Ella flailed, she stumbled backwards over the root of a tree and fell in a supine position. Before she had gained the wherewithal to get back up, the wolf which had been clinging to her boot pounced and in a flash was on top of her. The princess brandished her stick at the snarling menace but he gripped the wooden shaft in his teeth.

Another wolf sprung from Ella's right and bit her shoulder. It was all happening so quickly that she was no longer scared; she just watched it happen. The princess could only struggle on the ground, and it was a struggle that she seemed certain to lose.

But then she heard a male voice. "Tarva." The predator that had bitten Ella glanced around sheepishly and his confident pose receded. "Let her go!" commanded the voice from the woods. "Leino! Get off her!"

The wolf on the princess leapt off and both of the lupine assailants backed away while whimpering. Ella scrambled to her feet. The wolves that had surrounded Duncan also ceased their threatening behaviour.

A figure appeared in the moonlight. He was a tall man with a shaggy mop of hair on his head. He wore a leather tunic down to his knees and his muscular, veiny calves were visible below. His upper body was comparatively slender, though well-defined, and he held a spear in one hand. He waved the weapon and the several wolves retreated into the forest edge.

The man stepped closer and Ella could now see his face clearly. He had blue eyes, scars on both cheeks and stubble on his small chin. "Are you alright?" he asked in a dull tone.

"Just about," said the princess, breathing quickly as she clutched her wounded shoulder. Her heart was beating fast and she felt like she had cheated death. "I think you just saved my life."

The athletic figure shrugged. "Well, it was my fault for letting them chase you in the first place. I'm glad that you aren't too badly hurt."

Ella suddenly frowned. "These wolves are yours?" She glanced at her blood-stained dress.

"Indeed."

An expression of exasperation came over the princess, her large eyes glowering as she scowled. "Do you know who I am?"

"No, my lady."

"I am Ella Tundra, princess of Celtia and soon to be Queen!"

"Oh. Well I certainly did not know that." The shaggy-haired man put his spear down on the ground as a mark of respect. "Why were you travelling alone?"

"I was not! I was travelling with my dog!" Ella pointed at her bulldog and quivered.

The tall male stepped back. "I'm sorry, your highness. Is there anything that I can do to help? I can bandage that wound if you would like to come with me."

Ella's face contorted. "Why on earth would I want to come with *you?* I could have you imprisoned for letting your wolves attack me!"

A light appeared on the trail, growing brighter as it approached. The trotting of hooves and the whinnying of a horse were heard. An errant knight appeared, riding a white steed and holding a flaming torch in one hand. His hair was long and blonde and he wore a suit of armour with a navy cape. The mounted man looked down in surprise. "Is everything alright here?"

"*No!*"

"My lady, you're bleeding." The knight dismounted his horse. The princess clutched her shoulder and pouted at the handsome fellow before glaring at the shadowy figure by the woods.

"This vagabond's wolves attacked me! They stalked me along the trail!"

"Hey, I saved her from them."

"You saved me from your own wolves!"

"The lady is hurt," said the knight in a patronising tone. He pulled a vial from his pocket and poured its contents over Ella's wound before applying a white covering.

The wolf-man backed into the darkness with his animals while the blonde gent's strong hands applied the finishing touches to Ella's bandage. "Where are you going, miss?"

"My castle, home."

"You live in a castle?"

"Indeed. I am a princess. Ella of Tundra."

The knight fell into a stunned silence while Ella looked at the moon and fluttered her eyelashes. "Please accept my humblest apologies for not greeting your royal grace correctly." The armoured man kneeled.

"It's alright. You weren't to know."

"I am Sir Tarrent Lyonard of the Order of the Sacred Rose." He bowed. "Whatever your royal grace requires of me, I shall dutifully perform it."

"Well, I just need to get to my castle as soon as possible. I have an important day tomorrow and I need rest."

"Then I shall take you to your castle, if your grace would but tell me the way." Tarrent adjusted the saddle on his horse.

"There is a stone bridge not far from here," Ella said. "If you could take me there, I can walk up the hill to my castle, but your horse would struggle in such woods."

"Very well, your highness." The knight helped the princess onto the white steed.

"Thank you." Ella sat on the leather saddle and the knight positioned himself in front. "Don't go too quickly please," Ella requested as they trotted along the trail. "My bulldog cannot run very fast." Tarrent glanced down at the stocky canine and nodded.

Ella clung to the knight's broad, metal-plated shoulders, and tilted her head to gaze up at the starry sky. "I have not heard of the Order of the Sacred Rose. Are they based within this realm?"

Tarrent shook his head. "No. The Order stretches over many realms, but I am just passing through this one actually."

It was not long before they arrived at the limestone bridge. Tarrent looked into the woods on their left. "My horse would indeed struggle to get through those trees but we can try."

"It is alright," Ella said. "I would be quicker walking."

The knight alighted from his steed and helped the princess down. "Let me leave my horse here and walk with you to the castle then."

"Oh, don't be silly. We will be fine."

"Are you certain?"

Ella nodded firmly. "Yes, most certain. You have been very helpful, Sir Tarrent."

"At least take my torch. It will make your task much simpler." He offered her the flaming stick.

Ella's brow creased. "Will you not need it?"

"The moon is bright tonight and shines upon the trail, but in those woods, you would struggle without light."

"If you are sure." Ella happily received the torch. "Thank you."

Tarrent and Ella were confident enough that the vagabond's wolves had not followed them because they had not heard anything since riding. "I hope we meet again one day," said the knight.

"I hope so too. Goodbye, Sir Tarrent."

"Farewell," he said and pulled on the reins of his white horse. As he galloped away, Tarrent's navy cape flew up to reveal the back of his armour. A metallic engraving glinted in the moonlight and Ella's eyes widened. She saw a red rose with a golden snake coiled around its green stem.

"Wait!" Ella called, but it was too late. The knight vanished into the darkness of the night. The thumping of hooves quietened and then there was silence.

Ella muttered, glancing at Duncan, as they entered the woods to begin a gentle ascent. They had heavy legs and their bodies ached but they were eager to get home. The princess and the bulldog ambled through those same pleasant woods in which they had started their quest two days ago.

Owls hooted and Ella could soon see the faint lights of her castle through the thickets. Her walk turned into a jog and Duncan also bounded excitedly as he sensed that home was near.

As Ella strode towards the tower in which she had lived for most of her life, she thought about the rose engraved on the back of the knight's armour. It was strikingly similar in appearance to her key and Ella sighed in frustration at having missed the opportunity to ask about it. Had it been any other evening, she could have invited the handsome Sir Tarrent back to her castle. But tomorrow was the most important day of her life and the queen-to-be needed her beauty sleep.

When they reached the rear wall, Ella used a metal key to open an ivy-covered stone door. The weary pair ascended the spiral staircase and entered Ella's colourful bedchamber. The princess flopped on her pink bed and the bulldog slumped in his wicker basket. Both fell asleep at once.

CHAPTER 4 – ACCESSION

As Ella lay in her bed on the morning of her coronation, she wondered if she had dreamt the tempestuous events of the past days. But she received a sharp affirmation of their veracity when she moved her right arm, as a pain shot through her shoulder, and Ella groaned when she saw the blood stains on the bandage. Her limbs felt stiff and the queen-to-be wondered if she would even be able to walk. She placed a hand on her forehead and asked herself why she had gone through such an ordeal for the sake of visiting a crazy old man.

Yet it had been an adventure, and perhaps the greatest one of her life. The arduous jaunt had given Ella some truly rich experiences and unforgettable memories. Her father had always stressed the importance of real living, so it had been worth it in a way, even if her body told her otherwise. Ella may never again get to feel such rawness of being, because she was about to become a monarch, but she was sure that many interesting days lay ahead. The Coronation of Queen Ella Tundra of Celtia would begin at midday.

Ella dragged herself out of bed and glanced down at Duncan who was still asleep in his basket. The princess entered her marble bathroom, where she was pleasantly surprised to find that her maid had already poured her a bath. Jenny had a knack of knowing what Ella required without needing to ask. Ella dipped her hand in the water and found it to be just the right temperature, which put a smile on her face. She stepped in and sighed in relief; never had a bath felt quite so divinely satisfying.

As the covering on Ella's shoulder became soaked, it loosened and peeled off. She could now see her wounds, one large and one small, where the wolf's fangs had entered. Ella shivered in the water as the scene from last night flashed through her mind.

After bathing for an hour, the princess felt sufficiently cleansed and replenished. She wrapped a purple towel around her body and called for Jenny. The thin, dark-haired girl arrived within moments, and Ella asked her to apply a fresh bandage. Jenny dutifully obliged, not asking how the wounds were inflicted since it was not her place to. She wrapped a beige strap over Ella's shoulder and the princess thanked the maid before moving to her dressing room.

Ella looked through her wardrobe and selected a silky burgundy gown with puffy shoulder parts to hide her bandage. She also picked out two long violet gloves, a purple lace shawl and a favourite pair of red shoes. Ella applied a modest amount of make-up and wore an amethyst necklace above her bosom.

The coronation would take place in the capital of Livia, an illustrious city six miles east of the Tundra Castle. A line of gilded carriages waited in the front courtyard and Ella's heels tapped the cobblestones as she skipped to her elaborate coach, which was drawn by four horses; one brown, one grey, one black and one white.

Inside the velvety vehicle, the queen-to-be was protected by four Veraskan guards. These female warriors represented the elite force in Celtia and wore spectacular suits of bronze armour adorned with gold. Veraskan women were trained from infancy in the art of warfare and they were supremely skilled.

Ella's carriage was the middle in a train of thirteen, carrying various members of the privy chamber and royal household. Key figures such as the Lord Treasurer, Master of the Armoury and emissaries would attend, but so too would the lesser staff of servants, maids and castle runners. In one carriage sat a manicured fawn bulldog wearing a bejewelled red collar and purple cape. Duncan was flanked by his two personal minders for the day.

The coaches rumbled along the road, parts of which were paved and parts of which consisted of hard earth, as they passed woods, fields, lakes and valleys. Crowds of people lined the route near settlements, but the main throng waited in the city.

Just before midday, the procession reached Livia and entered a broad street teeming with jubilant crowds. Soldiers guarded barricades to prevent overflowing as the parade passed down the avenue and halted before a white pillared edifice. Ella held up the lower ends of her dress as she ascended the steps of the Marble Palace, which was the ceremonial centre of Celtia.

Ella soon emerged on the great balcony amid a fanfare of bugles and drums. She smiled and looked over the screaming swarms. "H-Hello." She swallowed. "I love this realm so very dearly." The delirium below reached a fever pitch, so Ella had to wait a while before continuing.

"I shall rule this kingdom – sorry, *queendom* – with the same diligence and prudence that my forebears showed. It is by those virtues that we, as a people, have elevated ourselves above the savage and formed this wondrous nation. My first aim is to continue the good work of my father, but beyond that, I wish to eliminate all strife and suffering." Ella grinned brightly and the masses threw their hats into the air.

The princess had never experienced such exultation before. Giddy on the deluge of euphoria, she glanced around at the various stone buildings and declared, "I find this city grey, but when I am finished, it will be *purple!*" Encouraged by the ecstasy of the crowd, Ella continued, "There will be purple towers, and purple horses, and purpl-" But the royal musicians began to play and their horns blared loud enough to drown out the new monarch's last few words.

Ella picked up the amethyst-jewelled staff which was the symbol of the Tundra dynasty, and now she was truly the Queen of Celtia. The large purple crystal glinted as the sun shone down upon the sovereign and her subjects. Ella waved the staff around as she basked in the adoration of her people, smiling so broadly and for so long that her face began to hurt. When the orchestra finished their coronation ode, Ella went back into the Marble Palace.

As the commoners commenced great feasts on the streets, the aristocracy sat down for their own grand banquet in the main hall of the palace. There were seven long tables arranged in parallel and one perpendicular at the front. In the centre of the high table sat Queen Ella on her throne, while a few seats along, a purpled-caped bulldog perched on a chair upholstered in velvet. Duncan would be served the same seven-course meal as the rest of the nobility. Two minders stood at his sides, prepared for the task of constantly cleaning the table around the bulldog, since he tended to eat his meals quickly and messily. They would also have to ensure that he did not eat too much of anyone else's food.

Before the feasting could begin, the new monarch had to choose her privy councillors, those men and women who would help govern the realm. The hall fell silent as Queen Ella unravelled a scroll with her violet gloves.

"Lord Treasurer ... Quintus Northwood."

A tall, thin man sporting a chestnut suit stood up from his seat and bowed. He had brown hair, a thick moustache and a pointed beard. "I thank her gracious majesty for retaining my services," said the Lord Treasurer. "May her realm be opulent and prosperous."

"Chief of the Justice … Dame Krista Kimber."

A buxom lady wearing a tight-fitting white dress got up, smiled and also thanked the new monarch for keeping her on. "May her realm be fair and equitable," said the Chief of the Justice.

"Master of the Armoury … Sir Terin Cormin."

A robust, grey-garbed man stood up and expressed his gratitude. "May her realm be impenetrable and indestructible," said the Master of the Armoury.

"Commander of the Standard … Dungeon Hark."

He was an athletic, middle-aged man with long raven hair and wore a ceremonial suit of armour in green and purple, the colours of Celtia. "May her realm be indomitable and mighty."

Dungeon was the head of the realm's regular army, which was considerably larger than the elite Veraskan unit, but inferior to it. Though the Veraskans were the foremost fighting force in Celtia, they were virtually a separate entity. The highland region of Veraska had once been an independent state, a martial society dominated by women. They had agreed to become part of Celtia, owing to the diplomatic skills of King Herald, the condition being that the fierce female champions received an important and well-rewarded role. Some would argue that the Veraskans were more akin to mercenaries but they had proved their worth many times in the decades since their incorporation. The blonde warrior chief of Nina Veraska sat at the high table in a sapphire dress, but she did not need to be appointed by the Queen because the Veraskans always chose their own leaders.

None of the names which Ella had read from her scroll so far had been surprising, as she had maintained the existing order chosen by her father; keeping those same tried and trusted officers. One position required new blood, however, because its previous holder had recently passed away.

"Bard Laureate…" said Queen Ella, curling her ruby red lips, "…Master Gullivander."

There was silence for a few moments. In the corner of the hall, at the far end of one table, a short blonde man stood up. He was dressed in a fancy green-and-gold tunic with blue pantaloons and brown fur boots. He threw his hands into the air and screamed loud enough to cause the Queen's bulldog to bark. The bard who had sung to Ella days ago in that little tavern in the woods had come to the coronation thinking that he might get to perform to the nobility if he was lucky. But now, he was the most important troubadour in the realm.

Gullivander screamed again, seeming quite drunk as he held his arms aloft with clenched fists. He ran through the aisles and slid across the marble floor on his knees to arrive before the high table. Queen Ella grinned while those of a stiffer composition appeared uncomfortable with the spontaneous show of unbridled elation. The bard gave an impromptu speech.

"May her reign be golden,
And her realm full of mirth,
Though our land is olden,
Today is a day of rebirth,
So let her smile embolden,
That star upon the earth,
To her we are beholden,
This queen of great worth."

Everyone in the room started to clap and cheer. Gullivander pulled his panpipes from his side and played a wonderfully graceful, floating tune. People danced to the bard's merry music, and suddenly the formal occasion erupted into something more akin to a common carnival.

Such festivities were already occurring in the streets of Livia as well as in the town squares and village greens throughout Celtia. There were feasts and celebrations, the likes of which the realm had never seen, as the beloved princess had just become monarch. The folk would eat, drink, sing and frolic through the day and night. At that time, it felt like a new golden age had begun.

It would not take Ella long to get to grips with being queen, for she knew how everything worked, having spent much time watching her father direct his privy councillors. Rather than move into the master room of the Tundra Castle, Ella chose to make the traditional bedchamber of the monarch a permanent memorial to King Aelfwoad. The new queen retained her pink-and-purple bedroom, where she had lived for most of her life and become quite attached to.

A splendorous onyx hall in the castle represented the high chamber of monarchic power. The varnished surfaces displayed an array of orange, red, amber and black bands which streaked across the floor and walls. There were eight pillars, four in a row on each side of the rectangular hall. The centrepiece was a gilded oak throne with red cushions, before which was a sparkling fountain and a great window. These gave the monarch plenty to look at while sitting on her throne, whether the calm running water of the fount or the forest outside through which animals roamed.

In this onyx hall, Queen Ella would spend much of her time ruling the realm. Here, she would listen to and direct her privy councillors. Merchants would seek to strike trade deals and emissaries would bring tidings from distant lands. It was a busy life, but much of it was spent sitting down, which made Ella all the more happy that she had enjoyed many adventurous days as an unfettered princess.

Musicians, actors, poets and the Bard Laureate would sometimes entertain the enthroned monarch. Servants would bring a steady supply of food and drink, though Ella would eat most of her main meals in the dining chamber. Whenever the Queen was in the onyx hall, three armoured Veraskan women would stand at the edges in case a sudden threat emerged.

On the morning of the third day of Queen Ella's reign, a young messenger came with some exciting news. The dark-haired boy went down on one knee as he read out his message.

"Your Majesty Queen Ella Tundra of Celtia, I bring news from the realm's finest adventurer. Ronwind Drake has arrived in Port Hope and his ship carries a cargo of seven treasure chests. He has discovered a new world far away, on the rim of the Azure Ocean, and it is a land rich in gold, silver and jewels. Captain Drake would like to personally show your majesty the treasures that he has acquired."

Ella's blue eyes glinted and she waved a hand of approval. "Tell him that I wish to see those treasures, good messenger. I will send carriages to collect them with Veraskans providing protection along the way."

The boy nodded and ran off, his thick mop of hair bouncing as his leather shoes tapped the hard floor. Three carriages soon departed the Tundra Castle, containing the Lord Treasurer Quintus Northwood and six Veraskan guards.

The sun reflected off the warrior women's shapely armours which covered most of their torsos. They wore large shoulder pads and metal skirts but their arms and legs were more exposed to allow for freedom of movement. Each Veraskan carried a bronze round shield on her back and a battle-axe at her hip. Helmet style was down to the individual but most included horns.

The outward journey passed without hitch and they reached Port Hope, eighteen miles south-east of the castle, in the early afternoon. This harbour town lay in the middle of a crescent-shaped bay which connected to the vast Azure Ocean.

The smells of salt and fish were overpowering as the carriages bumped along cobblestones towards the seafront. They saw the docked *Ptarmigan*, an impressive red-and-black galleon which belonged to the adventurer Ronwind Drake.

The vehicles parked on the edge of the pier, surrounded by various cargo boxes and rope pulley systems being operated by the busy dockers. Seagulls circled above, squalling and swooping to a nearby beach, while waves struck the stone pier and sprayed forth their froth.

The tall, bearded figure of Quintus got out of his carriage and looked at the ship swaying before him. Flanked by two Veraskan women, he walked up a ramp and boarded *The Ptarmigan*, stepping onto a deck cluttered with barrels, netting and nautical apparatus.

A man appeared from a cabin door and waved at the trio. He was unremarkable in appearance, short and stocky with curly, dull brown hair and a scraggly beard. His round face was red from being at sea for months and he wore a shabby leather garb. The Lord Treasurer, by contrast, wore a fine maroon suit with a cream hat, but he recognised the stout, scruffy man before him. "Ronwind," he said and offered a hand.

"Quintus, you old dog." The adventurer vigorously shook the stately man's hand. "Good to see you."

"How have you been?" asked Quintus.

"How have I been?" The short seaman laughed. "I couldn't even begin to tell you. We could speak all day and you would not learn one half of one twelfth of what I've seen, and even less of how I've been. But let me tell you one thing if nothing else... I have discovered a distant and uncharted land, a territory teeming with treasures!"

Ronwind ushered Quintus and the two female guards into his cabin. On the wall of the wooden chamber hung a portrait of the recently deceased King Aelfwoad, who had provided the ship and commissioned the voyage of exploration. On the floor lay seven chests of various sizes and shapes, one of which was open and full to the brim with glimmering gold pieces and green emeralds.

"Incredible," Quintus said as he touched his beard. "Do they all contain this much treasure?" Ronwind nodded. "Her majesty will faint when she sees these," the Lord Treasurer remarked.

The little captain grinned and poured two shots of whisky. "To the bejewelled glory of our new queen!" Ronwind declared as he raised his glass, and they toasted. The men threw their heads back and downed the malty spirit while the Veraskan women watched in silence.

"Now then," Quintus said. "Let us waste no time in bringing these treasures before her majesty so that she may see them before going to bed."

With the help of some cabin boys, they loaded the seven treasure chests onto the three carriages outside the ship. Quintus, Ronwind and the Veraskans embarked and the drivers pulled on the reins of the horses. The spiked wheels turned as they left the quaint port.

Laden with such cargo, the carriages moved at a slightly slower pace than they had done on the outward journey. Nonetheless, they made good progress until they entered a low wooded valley about halfway to the castle. In the middle of the track was a thick blockade of branches. This particular valley was notorious for its perils and treachery, which was one reason why the Veraskans had been provided, but they hoped that the obstruction was merely the coincidental result of fallen boughs.

As the carriages came to a halt behind the blockade, a group of hooded figures emerged from the woods on their right. A dozen dirty rogues stood in a line, clad in dark clothes, and then another dozen appeared on the left of the track. They carried an assortment of weapons; clubs, swords, pikes, axes and flails. Within moments, the bandits had spread out to fully encircle the three-carriage treasure train.

A thick-set brute, six and a half feet tall, raised his pike and spoke. "Ye shall not pass unless ye be stronger than we."

Quintus swallowed, his brow furrowing anxiously as he contemplated the best course of action. He looked at the treasure chests and considered striking a deal, perhaps offering the highwaymen two or three of the valuable cargo. But just as the Lord Treasurer raised his hand to utter a reply, six Veraskan women leapt simultaneously from the sides of the carriages.

In a flash of bronze and gold, the flurry of combat began. The ferocious female warriors spun and swirled, ducked and dodged and swung their axes. Metal struck metal as shouts and screams coursed through the low wooded valley. Like lionesses among cattle, the six women viscerally fought the much larger company of bandits.

Ronwind Drake, never one to be a bystander, jumped out of his carriage. The plucky adventurer drew his scimitar and surged forward, vanquishing one bandit before turning to slash at another. The three drivers followed his lead, all fit men who carried daggers, doing their best to help. Finally, Quintus unsheathed his sword and stepped into a gap between two Veraskans.

Those valiant eleven stubbornly resisted a force more than twice their number. The bandits began to waver, and half of their ranks had been cut down when their powerful leader fell amid a whirlwind of Veraskan axe-heads. Upon seeing the giant tumble, the remaining rogues panicked and fled into the forests. They staggered over branches and bushes as they escaped through those wildwoods wherefrom they had so boldly appeared not long before.

The six Veraskan women did not give chase. Emerald, Cherry, Heidi, Melody, Melissa and Blossom looked at one another to check that each was alright. They inspected their thick bodies which glistened with sweat, and found only a few scratches here and there.

They then cast their gazes on the men. Quintus and Ronwind panted, ruffled but not seriously hurt, while two of the drivers seemed fine, but one bled from his side. Emerald took out a healing kit and poured water over the young man's wound. She applied herbal salve, fixed a bandage and helped the ginger lad into a carriage.

The female champions groomed themselves, tying hair neatly into place and adjusting any armour which had fallen out of position. They cleared the crude blockade, chucking branches into the woods, and Melissa replaced the injured driver as the troupe recommenced their journey back to the castle.

CHAPTER 5 – A DISTANT PARADISE

When the three carriages reached the Tundra Castle, the injured fellow was taken to the medical ward and the treasure chests were carried into the onyx hall. The Veraskans returned to their all-female quarters for a well-deserved evening of leisure, while Quintus and Ronwind went to see their monarch.

The Queen was on her throne, playing with her bulldog who was stretched out on an adjacent couch. It was courteous for anyone entering the hall to wait for the monarch to speak before they did, so the two men looked down silently at the floor.

"Quintus, there is blood on your garb," Ella remarked as she stared at the Lord Treasurer. Her mouth was turned down in a slight frown and her expression did not alter when she glanced at Ronwind. The Queen seemed to disapprove of the appearance of both men, and even Duncan looked unimpressed.

"Indeed," Quintus said. "We were assailed by two dozen bandits on the return journey, your majesty."

"Oh." Ella gestured for him to continue his story.

"We were fortunate that the six Veraskans fought most heroically, and I can only commend your wisdom in choosing to send them. Myself and Ronwind also joined the battle, with the glory of our queen and realm as our inspiration. The three chaps driving the carriages assisted too and one of them was badly wounded. He was treated by the ladies and is currently recuperating in the hospice. Although heavily outnumbered, the eleven of us fought valiantly in order to protect your treasures, and we were ultimately victorious."

"Well, that would explain why your moustache is ruffled," Ella said and grinned. "It is usually immaculate, dear Quintus." The Lord Treasurer laughed somewhat nervously.

"Well done. I am very proud of you both." The Queen signalled to a castle runner. "Renton, see to it that the injured fellow eats like a prince tonight, and send some flowers to those Veraskans." The man nodded and scurried off.

"Now then." Ella looked at the weathered face of Ronwind Drake. "Introduce yourself to me, good fellow. I feel that we have met but I cannot recall your name."

The sun-burnt seaman swallowed. "I am Ronwind Drake,

adventurer and explorer extraordinaire. My voyage was commissioned by your father, King Aelfwoad, a year ago. I was tasked with finding virgin territories, and indeed I discovered an uncharted land on the far edge of the Azure Ocean. It is an exotic place full of bright feathers, sweet fruits, crystal waterfalls and turtle lakes. In this distant paradise, I found treasures beyond one's imagination."

Ella's eyes widened as she gazed at the chests on the floor.

"Hence," Ronwind continued, "I present seven chests full of treasure for your majesty's pleasure."

The Queen's face contorted in confusion. "I count only six." Ronwind and Quintus turned their heads and also saw six. They looked at each other in perplexity, and the Lord Treasurer turned to a servant. "Go and bring in the seventh chest!"

The lad ran off but returned empty-handed minutes later. "There is no seventh chest, sir."

Quintus snorted. "There were seven chests on those carriages! If you will excuse me, I shall go and get it myself."

But the Lord Treasurer could not find it either. "Your majesty," he said as he returned to the onyx hall. "The seventh treasure chest is indeed missing, and I can only think of one explanation. We were so overwhelmed and outnumbered by the bandits, that while we fought, the sly knaves must have managed to sneak away a chest. I take full responsibility for this failure, since it was my duty to check our cargo. I sincerely apologise, most gracious sovereign."

Ella blinked her long eyelashes and Ronwind mumbled a curse under his breath. He had travelled far and suffered the harshest conditions to gain those treasures and one had been stolen in their own backyard.

Quintus said, "I will assemble a taskforce and recover the seventh chest. It cannot have gotten very far."

But Queen Ella put a hand up. "Eh… Six treasure chests are enough for me. Perhaps now that those bandits are rich, they will no longer need to thieve from good people. Let them keep it."

The two men glanced at each other and nodded. The monarch turned her attention to the six chests on the floor. "Open them!"

Ronwind moved over to the haul and first slid the lid off a carved mahogany box. Ella's eyes glinted as she looked upon a sea of gold and gleaming green emeralds. The little adventurer next opened a square chest of light wood which was full of silver pieces.

Ronwind unlocked a third chest, similar in appearance to the second, and it contained red egg-shaped gems among more silver. Queen Ella picked up one of the deep carmine gems and bounced it on her palm.

The fourth chest was octagonal and constructed of engraved dark metal. Ronwind opened it to reveal a veritable trove of gold with several long purple gemstones in their midst. Ella gasped, her eyes going wide with cupidity. The mesmeric jewels seemed to sparkle from every angle and Ella examined one intently for several minutes. "This one shall adorn my new crown."

The fifth chest, a cylindrical trunk, contained many amber pieces. The sixth was the largest and made of red stone. Its complex opening mechanism consisted of several latches which Ronwind unlocked one by one. When the lid finally came off, Ella purred as she saw gold and jewels of every colour. Glimmering before the Queen's oceanic blue eyes were fire opals, rubies, sapphires, yellow crystals and pink diamonds. They looked like stars and planets shimmering among a golden ether.

"Ronwind, you little wonder! I am to make a new title, Royal Adventurer. I shall ensure that whatsoever equipment, ships and men you require are provided. Therefore, you may discover yet more wondrous worlds and bring me back more precious treasures. And whatsoever virgin lands you come across, you shall place a purple flag upon, bearing my insignia. I will endow you with a stately house and maids for when you are not away, and you will be the richest man in all the lands."

Ronwind went down on one knee. "It shall be done, your majesty."

"Good. Now take an item of your choosing from each chest."

Ronwind glanced over the shining treasures, keen not to upset the Queen by taking one that she desired, so he chose six rather small and dull pieces. Ella nodded and the stout man bowed before leaving the hall.

Queen Ella regarded her Lord Treasurer. He was in charge of the management of money and the distribution of wealth for government policies, and suddenly they had this abundance of riches at their disposal. "Quintus, what do you make of these treasures?"

"Your majesty, I believe that with such gold and silver, one could fund a year's worth of operations. One could purchase armies or acquire more land. One could enlargen one's sovereignty and further one's glory. Or one could improve one's realm by eliminating every wicked vagrant and evil bandit that wishes to do us harm."

The Queen raised a hand, so the bearded officer stopped talking. "I have a better idea. You will see to it that all of the silver and half of the gold are distributed to the poor people of this realm. Thus, they may purchase whatsoever food, shelter and other vital things that they require."

The Lord Treasurer appeared bewildered and the Queen continued, "For in my realm, there shall be no hunger or poverty." Ella scrunched her small nose, ignoring a request from Quintus to speak. "For it is not evil that creates criminals, but strife and suffering. It is the want for food and the lack of comfort that makes bandits out of boys and marauders out of men. But my realm is to be a realm full of happy and contented people who want for nothing."

Queen Ella paused before adding, "The rest of the gold, and the jewels, can go into our treasury until a time when they are required."

The Lord Treasurer seemed to bite his lip as he nodded. "Certainly, your majesty."

"Now ensure that these chests are locked away safely, and see to it that my new policy is put into action swiftly."

"Certainly, your majesty," Quintus said again. He gathered his servants to carry the chests to the castle vaults, but before they did, Ella picked out one jewel of each colour and took them with her to her bedchamber.

The Lord Treasurer went to his cosy candlelit office and sighed as he reclined in his leather chair. He was frustrated by the Queen's charitable plan for the relief of the poor. Executing such a lofty scheme would be more difficult than she seemed to realise. Quintus picked up a quill and set about trying to form some groundwork for the policy.

But he got nowhere and soon found himself staring out the window into the night's sky. As he gazed at the trees and the stars beyond, Quintus came up with a plan that had little to do with economics. He was aggrieved by the missing treasure chest. Given the contents of the other six, who knew what fortunes the seventh might contain? It could not have gotten very far either, as those bandits had been largely decimated. Whoever was in possession of that chest were likely few in number.

So, the Lord Treasurer decided that he would return to the scene of the battle with the Veraskan women from earlier. They would locate and recover the lost chest. Haste was the name of the game and the expedition would occur tonight. The bearded man leapt from his seat in excitement and walked through the corridor outside his office, where he gleaned from a servant that Queen Ella was tucked up in bed. This suited him because she had told him not to worry about the missing chest.

Quintus located the six Veraskans in their quarters and told them of his plan, pretending that he had the Queen's approval. He chose to take four of them, which was as many as one fast carriage could carry. It would be a mission of espionage more than of force, and the Veraskan ladies were not overly enthused, being forthright women of war, but they agreed that conducting it tonight gave them the best chance of success. They were also keen to redeem themselves after their self-perceived failure to protect the cargo earlier. To sweeten things, Quintus offered each of them a small share in the spoils.

The Lord Treasurer and the four female warriors set off in a carriage in which they were packed rather tightly together. Quintus wore dark attire and a tight black cap which made him look a bit like a bandit. The Veraskans wore studded leather armour rather than their usual heavy plates, but they brought their axes and shields.

The carriage sped along quiet roads and reached the low wooded valley after midnight. A torch hung from either side as they moved down the track and stopped at the location of today's skirmish. Quintus, Emerald, Heidi, Melissa and Melody got out and began to skirt the woodlands. The forest here was thick, which made it probable that the bandits had used a trail, and it was not long before they found one. Emerald called the others to show a surprisingly clear-cut path on the south side.

They proceeded quickly along the trail which was verged by brambly thickets. Quintus walked in the middle of the four Veraskans, two of whom held flaming torches. A garlicky smell intensified as they penetrated deeper into the forest.

After half an hour, the track descended into a narrow gorge. Vines covered the steep walls, through which roots poked, and moss-covered boulders hung overhead. A thin, starry strip was all that could be seen of the sky, but it disappeared as the five entered a cave.

Their footsteps echoed, as did the soft hiss of their flames, and they treaded cautiously. The rocky corridor twisted and turned before widening into a vast, dark cavern. The group stopped momentarily and listened to the eerie silence within the jagged chamber, interrupted only by a periodic dripping. When they proceeded forward, they noticed something shimmering on their left.

They realised that it was a metal padlock hanging on front of a rectangular chest. "*Aha!*" Quintus remarked gleefully, unable to contain his excitement at having located their objective.

Then they heard voices coming from further down the cavern, sounding like people waking up, probably as a result of Quintus's utterance. The five drew their weapons and Melissa waved her torch around as they walked towards the sounds.

The sphere of the flame's glow illuminated two figures; a short, hunchbacked fellow wearing a cowl and a young man sitting on a mat, rubbing his eyes. When the cowled figure saw the axe-heads, he immediately held his hands up. "Hey, wait!" He showed his palms to prove that he was unarmed and his friend did the same. These lads were clearly not interested in a fight.

Fire danced beneath the lengthy, bearded face of Quintus Northwood. "Where did you get that chest?"

"It's yours, I know it is," said the small fellow. "Take it, please. We could nay even open it. I was just doing what I was told."

"You robbed it from our carriages earlier, didn't you? In fact, I think I recognise him." Quintus pointed his sword at the other bandit.

"We did." The little rogue was almost crying. "We were just following orders, but most of our men are dead now. Look, we're sorry. Please take it."

Quintus was about to respond when they heard footsteps from behind. "If that's one of your men, call him off now, or I'll slay you on the spot!" the Lord Treasurer threatened.

"I thought it was one of yours."

"Don't play games with me boy!"

"Wait," said Emerald. "Listen."

They fell silent and heard sniffing and grunting. Then a terrifying and carnal roar resounded through the pitch black chamber. The little rogue screamed while the Veraskan women waved their torches and made noises to try to scare the hidden beast away. The echoes of the cavern made it difficult to discern exactly where the monster lurked.

The bandit who had been sitting down suddenly shrieked as he was dragged into the darkness, and the other dashed towards the Veraskans for their protection.

"What the heck is it?" Quintus queried.

"A bear most likely," the little rogue replied while cowering behind one of the powerful women. They heard more footsteps as another creature entered the cavern, making similar sounds to the first.

"We are not trained to fight bears," Melissa stated. "And these torches are about to die."

The bandit whispered, "Follow me." He moved towards the wall and disappeared through a crack. Melissa followed, and Emerald, Quintus, Heidi and Melody went in too.

They found themselves in a small chamber through which a whistling wind swirled. The chilly breeze came in via a chasm on the far side, and the remaining torch flickered out. "Is that the forest out there?" asked Quintus, squinting.

"No," said the little rogue. "That's the sea. We're in a cliff."

Melissa leaned out of the chasm and her braided blonde hair blew back. A shooting star flew through the night's sky as waves crashed against rocks far below.

"How's your climbing?" asked the bandit.

"Not great," Quintus said.

"It might be our only way out."

"How far is it to the top of the cliff?" asked Melissa.

"Only two dozen feet, but it's two hundred feet to the sea."

"Have you climbed it before?"

"Aye, once."

"Then let's do it. I don't fancy being mauled to death." The other Veraskans agreed. They could still hear the snorting and shuffling of two large animals in the adjacent cavern.

"What about the chest?" Quintus questioned.

"We can collect it tomorrow," Melissa said.

The little rogue murmured, "I can't guarantee that it will be there tomorrow. Other bandits use these caves."

"Then I am not leaving without that chest," Quintus affirmed. "Not after all we have been through."

"Good luck," Melissa said and squeezed into the chasm.

"What are you doing? Get that chest!" the Lord Treasurer

demanded, but the blonde woman disappeared out of view as she started to climb the cliff. Quintus turned to the others. "One of you can tie the chest to your back. It's only small."

"We already carry our shields," Emerald said. "Why don't you carry it?"

"You're the professionals," Quintus snapped, "you carry it!"

"We are professional soldiers, sir, not professional plunderers," Emerald retorted, and went through the chasm.

Quintus uttered a curse. He decided to risk the beasts prowling in the main cavern and retrieved the chest. Its metallic exterior scraped against rocky walls as he hurriedly returned to the breezy antechamber. "It's really not that heavy. Fine. If you tie it to my back, I will carry it."

Melody and Heidi reached into their packs and pulled out some rope. They removed their leather belts and managed to fasten the chest onto Quintus's back using the ropes and straps.

"Just copy me pal," said the bandit as they scrambled through the chasm. Cold winds hit the bearded officer's face as he looked over the sea and craned his neck to observe the little rogue scaling the cliff.

Quintus began to climb using the same nooks and holds. His cap blew off and loose rocks fell as he dragged himself up, inch by inch, in the most laboured of manners. He felt a sense of elation as he neared the top, and Melissa and Emerald reached down to help him over the edge.

But just as he was being hauled to safety, the chest slipped free from his back. Quintus turned his head and gaped as the metallic box tumbled through the air, narrowly missing Melody ascending the cliff. The rectangular container rotated as it fell two hundred feet to the sea and only the faintest splash could be heard as it finally entered the dark deep. Quintus gazed down in numb silence.

CHAPTER 6 – THE SEVENTH WONDER

Queen Ella had recently decided that her realm would hold a great midsummer carnival, which would be the most marvellous event that the world had ever seen. Every monarch and emperor would be invited and no expense would be spared. The World Fayre would have multiple purposes and benefits. It was an opportunity to negotiate multilateral trade deals with other realms and enhance relations with other rulers. But most of all, the inexperienced queen was keen to demonstrate her competence and prowess to the world. Ever since her father had died, Ella had been worried that Celtia was more susceptible to invasion, as realms often were when a great ruler passed away. Foreign powers tended to view the new ruler, especially if she was a young woman, as weak and vulnerable. Ella wanted to prove that she was a strong, capable leader, and what better way to do so than by holding a global event in which she could meet all those mighty monarchs? Plus, she could show off her new crown which would be ready by then.

The World Fayre would be held over three days in the great plain, which was the only place large enough to accommodate it. Emissaries were despatched around the globe to spread word of this monumental meeting. The fact that Ella was already world-renowned made it more likely that distant heads of state, particularly male ones, would attend. Many had heard the ballads of her beauty and now they would get their chance to meet the famous maiden.

Word spread throughout the towns and villages of Celtia too, for this would also be an occasion for the happy people of Queen Ella's realm. Smiths forged decorations, woodworkers constructed great apparatus, weavers weaved vast tents, sculptors sculpted statues and bards wrote plays just for the spectacle. There was never any shortage of work available during the early months of summer and there was enough gold in circulation to pay for it all thanks to Ronwind's discoveries. The nation was united in preparation and there was a buzz as Celtia would become the centre of the world for a few days.

Two weeks before the World Fayre, the Queen received word that Ronwind Drake wished to talk, so she arranged a meeting in the onyx hall. Ella sat on her throne and Duncan reclined on his couch as the stout adventurer entered the majestic chamber.

Ronwind looked a lot better than he had done after returning from his escapades on the high seas. His face was no longer red and blistered, his hair was now clean and combed to one side and his small beard was trimmed. He wore a pretentious outfit consisting of a cream suit with gold buttons, a lavender ruff around his neck and fawn suede high boots.

"My glorious queen." Ronwind bowed. "I come to your majesty with two exciting proposals. Well, one that is very exciting and one that is slightly exciting."

Ella waved her hand. "Then let us begin with the very exciting proposal."

"I have heard from knowledgeable sources that there exist magnificent riches in the cloud realm above us." Ronwind gestured to the ceiling. "These celestial treasures are beyond anything to be found on this terrestrial plane."

Queen Ella's big blue eyes keenly watched the flamboyant little man, who continued, "It so happens that the brilliant engineer Astronaemius is constructing a volitant vessel. He has been working on it for years, and it is near completion, but he is short on funds. His invention will be capable of floating to the skies and reaching the great cloud realm above. In such a ship, I could go up there, plant your purple flag and, with my skills of exploration, I could locate the sublime treasures and bring them back to your majesty. Therefrom, not only would you be richer than anyone on Earth, but would henceforth be known as Her Majesty the Cloud Queen, Ella Tundra the Heavenly Wonder, Esteemed Empress of the Skies."

Ella appeared speechless and bedazzled, staring at the plucky adventurer with wide, unblinking eyes as she considered his words. They sounded almost too fantastical to be true, but this man had already surprised her by bringing more gold than she had ever seen and gemstones which she never knew existed.

"Your proposal is remarkable, Mister Ronwind, and I am quite dumbfounded. Yet who am I to question it? For you have already surpassed the boundary of the extraordinary, and in past endeavours have exceeded yourself. Indeed, you have proved to me that you are the greatest adventurer in the land, if not the world."

"Therefore, I will see to it that this special vessel is completed, so that you may fly to the cloud realm, claim it in my name and discover its unworldly treasures. And if you succeed in this task, you will of course be bestowed with a reward befitting of an Emperor of the Clouds."

Ella smiled. "Moreover, I know of just the stage from which you can launch your celestial quest. The World Fayre at midsummer. When you soar into the skies, everyone will witness the heavenly splendour of my realm and the ingenuity of my people. So then, I will ensure that Astronaemius's invention is completed with utmost haste."

Ronwind was overjoyed. "Your majesty's wisdom is truly of divine origin. We are blessed to be governed by one so enlightened. I will surely repay the faith shown in me."

The Queen nodded. "Now then, what was your less exciting idea?"

"Ah yes," the short sailor said. "On the return leg of my recent voyage, I passed a small island, some ninety miles from our eastern shores. As far as I am aware, this island is uninhabited and uncharted, as I have never seen nor heard of it. I am planning on setting out to explore it tomorrow and it should only take a day to reach in my galleon. I was wondering if your highness would like to join me. Of course, I understand if she is too busy, but this island really ought to belong to Celtia. We are the nearest realm and what better way to claim the territory than by placing the dainty feet of our most glorious monarch upon it?"

Ella raised an eyebrow. "That is much more than a slightly exciting proposal, Ronwind. Why, that is almost as exciting as your first proposal. I haven't been on a ship since I was a young child. I would certainly like to join you, so now let me think... I suppose we would need three or four days at most to allow for any unexpected hitches. I think my realm should be able to survive without me for that long."

"Superb," Ronwind said. "Is tomorrow fine with your majesty?"

"Indeed. The sooner the better. The closer we get to midsummer, the more I will be occupied with preparations for the World Fayre. In fact, the only consecutive days I am likely to be free are in this week. So let us leave Port Hope tomorrow morning for our aquatic adventure."

"Wonderful. Now I shall spend the rest of the day ensuring that my vessel is fit for a queen!"

"See you tomorrow," said Ella, and the adventurer went on his way. The Queen got off her throne and Duncan leapt off his couch to follow his mistress out of the hall, when Quintus suddenly appeared.

Ella stopped and sighed. "What is it, Quintus?"

"Sorry to disturb your majesty," the Lord Treasurer said hurriedly. "I just had a quick question concerning your policy for the charitable relief of the poor. In terms of the economic parameters re-"

The Queen put a hand up. "Do not worry about that for now, Quintus. I have a more important request. From tomorrow, I will be at sea for a few days, and I need someone to rule the realm in my absence."

Quintus looked stunned. "Your majesty, I am most humbled."

But Ella continued, "So I have decided to put Duncan on the throne. Now, since he is a dog, he won't be able to give spoken responses to people's questions. So, your job is to draw up a charter which details the meanings of his various facial expressions, barks and head movements."

Quintus glanced at the gormless, droopy-faced bulldog.

"I think you know him well enough," said the Queen, "but if you feel that you do not, then I suggest spending some time together now." She handed him Duncan's red leash, and the mutt's big brown eyes stared up at the bearded officer. "I need to go and prepare," Ella said, leaving the pair in the hall.

The monarch sent a courier to invite her Bard Laureate on the voyage, because she would probably need some entertainment. Queen Ella told her maids what possessions to pack and went to bed early.

The next day, she arose at dawn and put on a dark blue dress. She left the castle in a fast carriage with three Veraskans, who would also come on the ship. They reached Port Hope in the late morning and rumbled towards the pier, where they saw Ronwind's red-and-black galleon glistening in the sun, sails spread and ready to depart.

When they boarded the ship, the Queen and her female guards were greeted on deck by Ronwind and Gullivander. The stout sea captain wore a dark green outfit while the blonde bard sported an indigo-and-jasmine garb. The two men bowed and Ella cast a scrutinising eye around the deck, which she found to be quite spotless. A boy poured a bucket of water over the side of the boat while another put a mop away.

"Her majesty's room." Ronwind took his royal guest into the main cabin, normally for the captain. On the wall of the wood-panelled chamber hung a portrait of King Aelfwoad, which put a tear in Ella's eye but at least made her feel at home. The musty cabin had a small navy bed, a low table and plush furnishings.

When Ella emerged from her room, Ronwind was at the wheel of the ship which had begun drifting through the waters. The others watched from the rear of the vessel as Port Hope shrunk into the distance. The Queen had never seen her realm from this perspective before and she could soon make out the top of her castle on a faraway hill.

The sky was blue and the sea calm. "Perfect conditions," Ronwind said. "We should reach the island by dawn, which will give us a full day to explore."

"Won't you need sleep?" Ella asked.

"Of course," said the captain as a cool breeze swept over them. "But my first mate Dean will take over in the evening. He'll be sleeping from now until then."

"How many crew do you have?"

"Four. A cook and a couple of cabin boys as well as Dean. They're probably working in the hull right now or are too scared of those Veraskan ladies to come out on deck." Ronwind chuckled.

Ella smirked and looked at the three armoured women, who were gazing across the ocean while Gullivander seemed to be trying to initiate conversation with them. "Did you not bring any guards?"

Ronwind shook his head. "No, your majesty. We won't need any."

"What if we encounter pirates or hostile people on this island?"

"No pirate would dare attack *The Ptarmigan*," Ronwind declared while turning the wheel. "There is no vessel in the Azure Ocean more feared than this one! And as for the island, I am certain that no-one lives there. It's too small and wouldn't have fresh water."

Queen Ella went over to Gullivander and the Veraskans. The bard was strumming on his lute and singing to the women but they were barely paying him any attention.

"To hear your fiery battle cries,
Soaring through the summer skies,
To gaze upon your glistening thighs,
Makes m-"

When he saw Ella, he trailed off and his fingers played the wrong chord. "I was just-… I mean, hello your majesty." The bard bowed to the Queen and the Veraskan women grinned.

"Play me some melodies, Gully."

As the bard performed, a refreshing current caused Ella's golden-brown hair to flow back and she looked over shimmering waters.

"She is that ocean breeze,
How softly does she glide,
Floating above the seas,
Drifting across the tide,
She never fails to please,
Fresh-faced and blue-eyed,
Her hand I want to squeeze,
To see her smile so wide,
Though she makes me freeze,
My thrill I cannot hide,
She may weaken my knees,
But such bliss I feel inside."

Ella smiled, and the hours passed quickly as she listened to the masterful bard's marvellous music. The potent freshness of the sea air had a tranquilizing effect, and the Queen eventually felt the need to lie down. She went into her cabin and drifted off.

When she roused, it was late evening. "Ah," Ronwind said as she stepped onto deck, "her majesty has awoken just in time to see this glorious sunset." Ella looked at the horizon and saw a magnificent pink splendour as the sun sunk into the ocean.

"Dinner will be ready soon," the stout captain said. "Perhaps we could dine in her majesty's cabin? The one downstairs is rather dank."

"Certainly," Ella said and rubbed her eyes, still slightly groggy after having slept for a while.

Ronwind, Ella and Gullivander went into the cabin and sat around a candlelit table. The Queen turned to the adventurer. "Tell us about your voyage around the world, Ronwind."

"Where to begin," he mused as the ship's cook came in with a starter of vegetable soup. "How about the time we saw a ghost ship in the middle of the Azure Ocean?"

"A ghost ship?" Gully said, glancing out the window at the dusky sky.

"That's what we call a drifting, abandoned ship," Ronwind explained. "Why there was no-one on it, your guess is as good as mine. It was as big as my vessel, stocked with food, wine and cargo, but not a single person."

"How did you know it was stocked with all of those things?" asked the bard.

"Because we boarded it. We saw the ship sailing abnormally so we decided to try and help. When we drew close, we realised that there was nobody at the wheel. So we went aboard, searched every room, cupboard, nook and cranny, but found not a soul. We then took a good deal of their provisions, since we were running low ourselves."

"You plundered their ship?" asked Ella with a slight frown.

"Whose ship? There was no-one on it!" Ronwind said. "They must have all jumped deck for some reason or another. It's one mystery that I will never solve."

The Queen nodded. "Where is that ship now?"

"Probably crashed on rocks or beached somewhere." Ronwind shrugged. The main course arrived on the table, pork with sweet potatoes and apple sauce. The three companions dug in to the hearty fare and drunk white wine. "Did I tell you about that time I freed those slaves?" Ronwind asked with his mouth full. The others shook their heads.

"We were on the eastern fringe of the Azure, looking for somewhere to get fresh water, so we moored at a cove. We stepped ashore and met some locals in a jungle. We made friends, even though we were hardly able to communicate. They took us up a tall tree, on a ridge, and from there we could see the two great oceans of the world. We were on an isthmus, you see, and it was a stunning sight."

"They led us to a fort," Ronwind continued, "an outpost of the Assyrian Empire, where they held slaves, including ones captured from our friendly tribe. So we overpowered the guards, who never expected to see anyone wearing armour out there, because the locals wore animal skins. We opened the gates and the slaves poured out. The tribe took us back to their mud huts and started worshipping us." He chuckled. "Eventually we got hold of the water we needed."

"Oh, that's a great story," Ella remarked with a smile.

When they finished their dessert of treacle tart with cream, Ronwind said, "We should try and get some sleep, as we'll want to be awake when we reach the island." The adventurer stood up and hugged both of his friends before leaving the cabin.

Ella turned to Gullivander. "Play me a few more tunes." The

Queen lay on her bed as the ship gently swayed. The bard took out his lute, strummed some dreamy melodies and softly sung.

"Oh Queen Ella of Tundra,
Let no-one put us asunder,
Your smile gives me such pleasure,
You are the most glittering treasure,
Oh Queen Ella of Tundra,
Worth more than any gold plunder,
A lady of luxury and leisure,
Yet kind and caring beyond measure,
Oh Queen Ella of Tundra,
You are the world's seventh wonder."

When Gullivander stopped playing, Ella seemed to have fallen asleep. The bard put his instrument away, blew the candle out and quietly left the room.

It was nearly dawn when the Queen awoke and still quite dark. She went out and saw Ronwind steering the wheel at the front of the ship, so walked up to him. The small captain jumped. "Heck, you frightened the life out of me there."

Ella grinned. "Don't worry, Ronwind. This isn't a ghost ship. Are we almost there?"

"Indeed, that is the island ahead of us." Ronwind put the side of a hand up to his brow and gazed at an outline.

"It doesn't look very big," said Ella, although it was not yet light enough to get a clear picture.

"I know. The darkness has that effect," Ronwind reasoned. "The sun will rise in a matter of minutes."

They heard waves breaking against rocks as the ship approached the island, and Gullivander came onto deck. "That's the island?"

Ella smirked at Gully and glanced at Ronwind. "It will look bigger when we have more light," she said.

But as the sun illuminated the oceanscape, it became apparent that the island was no more than a rock, roughly square-shaped and forty feet across. In its centre, a seal lay, smiling happily at the visitors.

Ronwind frantically scanned the horizon, but there was nothing else in this vast blue sea. "It-... I-... It looked larger than that! It did!"

Ella and Gully stared at their captain. "What was the weather like when you saw this 'island'?" questioned the bard.

"It was foggy. But…" Ronwind sighed. "Alright. It looks like I made a mistake. There clearly is no island." He hung his head. "I'm sorry for wasting both of your time by bringing you on this voyage."

"Maybe it was a ghost island," Ella quipped.

Gully chuckled. "Not to worry, Ronwind. I've really enjoyed this voyage and I'm sure that her majesty has too. It has been interesting to experience life at sea."

Ronwind nodded slowly. "I might as well turn this vessel around now."

"Wait," Ella said. "Let's at least step onto the skerry, after coming all this way. I want to say hello to that seal."

"We risk dashing the ship on rocks if we get any closer, your highness," said Ronwind. "But if you want to swim, go ahead, and we will wait."

Gully grinned while Ella looked down at the waters. "Eh, that seal doesn't look too friendly actually." She shrugged and the others chortled. As the sun rose, *The Ptarmigan* turned and began to make its way back to Celtia.

In the late morning, Gullivander said, "Hey, look at that," and his companions turned their heads south. In the distance was a great fleet of crimson and gold ships, above which a convoy of white clouds seemed to sail upon the blue firmament of the sky.

"Praetorians," Ronwind murmured. "That is a large fleet. They must be invading somewhere, or returning from an invasion."

Queen Ella and Gullivander stared in wonder at the sparkling armada of twenty vessels. "The sun never sets on their empire," Ronwind remarked.

"What a glorious sight," said the bard. "Is it true that the Praetorians possess the most powerful empire in the world?"

"It is greater than the next two combined," Ronwind answered. "Praetorians – and I've met a few – like to boast that they've conquered everything worth conquering. But that's just bravado. Some day, they will want a foothold on our continent too."

Ella frowned. "If they did that, then all the nations on our continent would unite against them. No empire can rule the whole world, and every empire falls eventually. Often it is when they seem to be at their strongest that they collapse. That is what my father once said."

Ronwind nodded. "Wise words, your highness. Imperial hubris, as they call it. It would only take one bad emperor to destroy everything that his forebears created."

"Oh," Ella said suddenly. "You are both most knowledgeable. Do you know anything about the Order of the Sacred Rose?"

"I've heard the name," Gully replied but could offer nothing more.

"No-one knows anything about the Order of the Sacred Rose," Ronwind said as he continued to steer the ship.

"So you must know something about them then," Ella said.

Ronwind chuckled. "Only what I've heard from others. But some say they are just a legend."

"I think they are real, because I met a knight of the Order of the Sacred Rose, not long ago." The Queen turned to the bard. "Gully, remember when I first met you, on my way to Saxophyllus? On the return trek, I encountered a knight of that order. On his armour was an engraving of a rose with a golden snake around its stem." Ella reached into her pocket and pulled out her special key. "It looked very similar to my key, except that this isn't a snake." She rubbed her thumb along the smooth gold spiral.

"What's that for?" asked Ronwind as he glanced at the key.

"I don't know. I found it," Ella said, not wanting to talk about the prophecy. "But tell me what you have heard about the Order of the Sacred Rose."

Ronwind stared at the ocean. "Well, they call themselves a chivalric order but they seem more like a cult to me. I understand that their main purpose is to find this 'sacred rose', which must have some kind of power. I'm not sure, and I'm not sure if they're sure either. But they spend their days looking for this one rose, or perhaps it's a rose bush... I don't know."

Ella listened intently. "Do you know what the meaning of the snake is?"

"They believe that a serpent guards the 'sacred rose', I think. But I'm just going on hearsay here. That's all I know about them. What was the knight you met like?"

"He was courteous, chivalrous and handsome. Everything that I would expect a knight to be really."

For the rest of the journey to Port Hope, the trio chatted idly, ate and drank. When Queen Ella returned to the Tundra Castle, she found that her realm had not suffered any mishaps under the astute stewardship of her bulldog.

CHAPTER 7 – THE WORLD FAYRE

On the evening before the World Fayre, Ella and her entourage travelled to the great plain. Most of the tents were already erected and the Queen wanted to sleep in hers tonight to ensure that she was the first to arrive in the morning. She was led to a grand purple pavilion which dwarfed all those around it.

Inside this colossal tent, there was everything that a monarch could require; a hall with a throne where Ella would greet the leaders of the world, a velvet bedroom with a four-poster bed, a mahogany dressing room, a brass bathroom, guard quarters and a flower garden. The pavilion was so tall that to look at the apex made one feel dizzy, but if one did, one would see the finest cloths in many shades of purple, pink and red. Cerise sheets, mauve silks and violet linens were draped so loftily that there appeared to be elevated corridors and secret chambers, but no human moved up there; only the white doves which flew above the oak tree in the middle of the tent.

Ella hopped onto her luxurious bed and drew the translucent plum curtains across its sides. As the monarch slumbered, Veraskans would patrol the labyrinth of corridors throughout the fabric pavilion. Falling asleep within such a paradisiacal tent was not easy, but Ella eventually managed to drift off.

On the day of midsummer, the scene on the great plain was truly something to behold. Tents of every size, shape and colour stretched for miles, like gigantic flowers rising from the grassy meadows. The majority of Celtia's population was gathered in the plain, as the World Fayre was not only an event for the elites of the world but also a celebratory occasion for the contented commoners of Ella's queendom.

Hogs roasted on spitfires and peasants encircled wooden round tables. There were food tents, drinking holes and gambling dens, while theatrical marquees offered plays, music and poetry. There were competitions and contests of every kind, from thespian duels to knightly jousts. From the first light of dawn, the most eager had begun their revelry and they would make merry for the next three days.

A palisade wall separated the area designated for the sovereigns from the carnival of the sprawling masses. The tents in this protected section were much more elaborate, and sleeping quarters had been arranged for all of the rulers and their companies.

The elites came in great throngs identifiable by their colours and costumes. A few had brought small armies for safety while most were accompanied by modest bodyguards. Some monarchs were carried on litters while others came in carriages. The vehicles of lesser leaders were pulled by a few horses while more important rulers sat in huge coaches drawn by twelve stallions. Unique fanfares of horns and drums signalled the arrival of particular sovereigns and some were heralded by their own anthems. Above this stupendous commotion waved many flags of different emblems.

Ella's vast pavilion, that circular purple tent with a golden sphere on top, was in the middle of the designated section. The Queen had been sitting on her throne since the early morning, determined to greet every sovereign, no matter how small or great their realm. Ella wore an elegant violet dress and held her royal amethyst staff. Upon her golden-brown hair sat her newly forged crown. The work of the finest goldsmiths in Celtia was both magnificent and garish. Among four golden arches lay four purple gemstones and on top of the crown sparkled a red ruby.

The first to enter Queen Ella's tent was Queen Nicola of Mayra, a realm which bordered on the south of Celtia. Ella and Nicola knew one another, having met several times when they were princesses, but they had not seen each other for a few years. At twenty-one, Nicola was slightly younger than Ella and almost as pretty, with long curly brown hair and large hazel eyes. She wore a simple but stately white dress and a pearly tiara. Ella embraced her friend, kissing Nicola on both cheeks, which she returned.

"It is lovely to see you again," said Queen Nicola. "I offer the deepest condolences for your father, a great king who always strove for good relations with his neighbours. Our two realms have known peace for generations now and we have both prospered as a result. I bring a gift to show my appreciation for your majesty, and I hope that the harmony between our dynasties may last forever."

Nicola's servants brought forth a sizeable tapestry which they unravelled before Ella. It displayed a history of both nations intertwined as one, depicting their rise and coming together.

"This is most wonderful. What a unique and beautiful gift. Thank you very much, Queen Nicola. I will put this tapestry on the wall of my Marble Palace, so that others may see it and know of our bond. As long as I sit on the throne of Celtia, there will be peace between our realms."

"Hopefully I will see you later," Queen Nicola said, "if you are not too busy." She curtsied before leaving the tent, to join in with the festivities occurring outside.

A dark-haired man in a navy tunic entered the tent and gave Queen Ella a bottle of white wine. Duke Laurent of Carpagne did not chat for long because he was a shy and polite young man who had seen the queue of important rulers forming behind him. Next came Margrave Melton of Bolbrack, a stocky, bald, beardy man in a grey herringbone suit. He did not have much to say for himself either, simply greeting the queen and giving her a box of pipes and tobacco. Ella politely thanked him for the gift which she was unlikely to ever use.

A handsome mature gentleman, who seemed to have a bit more charisma about him, then entered Ella's pavilion. He wore a chocolate tweed suit with a matching red-feathered hat, and his grey moustache was the largest Ella had seen. He had a sharp face, an aquiline nose, and was thin and stiff-backed, which made him appear taller than he actually was. Leaning on his walking stick, the old man constantly turned his head over his shoulders as he seemed to inspect every object in the room. When he finally looked at the enthroned monarch, he appeared startled.

Ella smiled towards the quaint fellow. "Greetings."

The moustached man clutched at the front of his jacket and then at his pockets, as though he had forgotten something, while his expression remained one of bewilderment. "Oh, hello," he said, apparently just noticing the queen before him despite having already looked at her. "What a beautiful crown," he remarked, squinting his brown eyes. "You must be Queen Ella." He stepped forward and offered a hand.

It was not the way most people greeted a queen, but Ella received his hand and shook it. "Thank you, and indeed; that is who I am." She stared at the man, still having no idea who he was.

The elderly chap put a hand on his mouth and another upon his hip before abruptly raising his eyebrows. "Viscount Elgar of Cosgrove." The ends of his hoary moustache bounced as he nodded his head. "I believe I met your father once, some twenty years ago. I am terribly sorry to learn of his passing away."

"Thank you, Viscount Elgar. Where did you meet him?"

"At a carnival, like this one actually, but nothing as spectacular. This is a most wonderful event that you have organised." As the gentlemen gushed with praise, a fawn bulldog suddenly bounded into the room, his tongue flailing as he panted.

"Duncan!" Ella called, but the bulldog charged straight for Viscount Elgar. Duncan was not supposed to be in here and the canine's minder came running through as he exclaimed, "He slipped his collar off!"

The excited mutt leapt up at the old man, almost knocking him over, but Elgar chuckled. "This must be the King." The viscount vigorously stroked the head of the bulldog.

Duncan's minder managed to attach the red collar and led him away. "Don't let that happen again please," Queen Ella stated. She did not want to see Duncan jumping up at any emperors, kings or queens. "Sorry about that," she said to Elgar.

"Not at all," the sprightly gentleman replied. "What a fine chap! I have six dogs myself. Duncan must meet them some day."

Ella smiled. "Oh, what breeds?"

"A cocker spaniel, a cavalier spaniel, a wolfhound, a mastiff, a bloodhound and a beagle. Anyhow, I shan't keep you, because you have a queue of admirers waiting outside." The viscount grinned and tipped his hat. "It has been a pleasure to meet you, Queen Ella."

"Thank you, Elgar. I will see you later."

Ella looked at the old man as he hobbled out of the room. There was something quite intriguing about him. He had brought no gift, nor used any of the courtly formalities, yet his aura seemed distinctly noble.

The enthroned monarch next greeted Queen Bethan of Morga. Long golden tresses fell around her ample bust and she wore a tight black dress with high heels. Her voice was husky and soothing, and her demeanour pleasant if a little haughty. Bethan gave Ella a silver necklace before another woman came in. Duchess Brady of Northaw had curly red hair, freckles upon her skin and a sky blue dress over her petite frame. She offered a gold ring and complimented Queen Ella on her opulent crown.

Over the course of the morning, many more minor sovereigns came to see Ella, and the pile of gifts next to her throne grew bigger.

Most of these rulers were of lesser status than the Queen of Celtia and some depended on her good grace to a certain extent. Ella was happy to see them all, but they did not interest her as much as those great emperors and mighty monarchs whom she was anxious to make favourable impressions upon.

The first of such rulers arrived amid a glorious fanfare. Drums beat powerfully to create a climax while horns blew. The nature of their tune could only be described as triumphal.

Six Praetorian soldiers entered the hall of Queen Ella's throne. The dainty monarch had heard tales of the legendary legionaries but never seen them with her own eyes. These were soldiers of such athletic prowess and military discipline that they were sometimes said to be invincible. They wore shining helmets crested by horsehair, segmented cuirasses protected their torsos and red capes hung on their backs. Veins bulged from their arms like the ideal warriors represented in statues. From their girdles hung strips of studded leather, bronze greaves covered their shins and cross-hatches supported the sandals on their feet. At the belt of each Praetorian was a sword, his *gladius*.

Their leader looked like a soldier, only even more impressive. An iron plate was moulded to the shape of his powerful chest and decorated with a golden engraving of eagle wings. Two tasselled pads adorned his shoulders, crimson sleeves hung to his elbows and gleaming gauntlets covered his forearms. He wore a red skirt, metallic boots, and a scarlet cape flowed behind him.

His face was handsome, with a prominent nose, thin lips and a sculpted chin. His eyes glowed of amber, and upon his dark hair was a crown of leaves. It was a beautiful thing that a man of such power, the pinnacle of human civilization, wore only a simple laurel wreath; like he represented the Earth itself and all of its plants, trees and flora.

"I am Gaius Romulus Caesar, Emperor of the Earth," he declared, raising his arms as though he had just released a bird from his hands. "My realm is boundless and my people number as the sand of the sea. My city is eternal and my dominion everlasting."

"My empire is the tree of the world. Every other nation of this planet depends on the fruit hanging from my branches. But if I am the world's tree, then you are the world's rose, Queen Ella Tundra. And though a tree stands tall and a rose creeps on the ground, our roots are buried in the same soil."

Ella appeared spellbound, frozen in her seat like a spectator watching a theatrical performance. Caesar clicked his fingers and two men brought forward a round object cloaked in red cloth.

As they removed the material, Ella's eyes widened. She gazed upon a bejewelled sphere, a glittering representation of the Earth. Each nation was cut of a particular gemstone; blue azurite for the seas and red beryl carved in the shape of Caesar's Praetorian Empire. Ella gaped as she saw her own realm represented by a tiny amethyst crystal. "I present this gift to you," Caesar said, amber eyes glowing above the lustrous globe.

"Th-Thank you," Ella uttered.

The august emperor went down on one knee. "If you ever need anything, I will provide it. If your realm is invaded, I will send my legions. If your land is famished, I will send my grain. If your treasury is empty, I will send my gold."

Ella's lips quivered as she tried to muster a response, but only a slight stutter came out. Caesar kissed the queen's trembling hand and then rose, turned and exited amid the same fanfare that had heralded his entry. Ella was left with the view of the Praetorians' red capes as they departed. She was in a daze, having barely said a word to the handsome emperor, but he had hardly given her opportunity to.

The monarch had to compose herself as another ruler entered the tent, a physically imposing man with a purposeful stride. He had an impressive red beard with a blonde moustache and a long scar on one cheek. He wore a garb of burgundy, an auburn cloak and a gold crown. A gilded sword clinked at the side of the man who was surrounded by several aides.

"Greetings, your majesty Queen Ella," he said in a gruff voice. "It is I, King Bosgald of Borra."

"Hello." Ella smiled slightly, seated on her throne and wielding her amethyst staff.

The robust man clenched a fist. "My land was once called the 'savage north', but we the 'barbarians' are a risen people. United now as one power, our realm grows in strength each year, and we are already the foremost nation on this continent."

Queen Ella listened to the monologue as she watched King Bosgald with an unmoving face. He continued, "I come here to show my respect for your realm and your dynasty. My land may be cold but

I bring these presents as a token of my warmth."

Some little boxes were handed to Ella, which she opened and saw an interesting range of curios; jewellery, perfume and other trinkets. "These are very nice indeed. Thank you ever so much, King Bosgald." Ella smelled one bottle of perfume which had a pleasant, woody scent. It was a fragrance more suited to a king than a queen, but she did not mention that.

Bosgald stepped in front of Ella, clearly hoping to get a kiss or an embrace, but she remained on her throne. She offered her dainty hand, and his lips touched her skin for several seconds before sliding away.

Shortly after the 'barbarian king' departed, a most peculiar parade came in. The fellow at the front of the group wore a giant fish upon his head. The gormless face of the dead sea creature pointed up, covering the man's hair, while its hollowed carcass hung over his back, silvery scales swaying as he walked. The strange figure wore a dark yellow ephod over light blue vestments. His grey beard was tiered by strings and cyan orbs hung from his ears. He carried a long staff topped by a sapphire sphere, and as he moved his hand, the sphere turned and made a high-pitched shimmering sound. Ella had never seen such a bizarre person before. Perhaps he was some sort of ceremonial figure or high priest.

After him came six armed guards who looked identical to each other, wearing blue-and-yellow uniforms with chainmail and peaked jonquil hats. They were followed by four servants carrying a teal-and-gold throne, upon which sat the rotund sovereign. He wore a turquoise lappet crown, and his sizeable beard hung in ringlets which gave the impression that a cluster of serpents grew from his chin. Cerulean baubles dangled from his earlobes and a black shadow surrounded his bulbous eyes. He looked at least fifty years old and his olive skin was wrinkled.

After several similarly-attired men entered, the blue-and-yellow procession halted. Ella scrutinised the immaculately decorated, exotic entourage, while the fat ruler's grey eyes stared blankly at her.

A small man stepped forward from the back of the group. "King Sennacherib of Assyria greets you," said the interpreter. "This is the first time he has set foot on Celtia, and he is impressed by what he sees."

Queen Ella nodded. "Thank you."

"He also brings gifts." Servants unravelled two animal skin rugs before Ella, one of a tiger and one of a lion.

"Oh. How lovely." Ella smiled politely and examined the furs.

"His Excellency hunted them himself," the interpreter declared and the large leader bounced on his throne.

"Wow. That's amazing. Well done." The rugs were placed on the floor and the feline predators' dead eyes stared up at the queen.

King Sennacherib tilted his head as he gazed upon the pretty maiden. He looked at her ostentatious bejewelled crown, of which purple was the dominant colour. Suddenly, his eyes narrowed and his placid expression became perturbed. The ruler said something to his interpreter and a heated dialogue followed in their foreign tongue.

"King Sennacherib finds the jewels of your crown most impressive. Do you know where they come from?"

"Thank you. Yes, I do. An adventurer of my realm found them in a distant paradise."

The interpreter relayed the information to his king, and they had another brief conversation before he addressed Ella again. "May His Excellency have a closer look at your crown? He is most intrigued by it."

"I suppose so." Queen Ella removed the elaborate headpiece and handed it to the man, who kneeled as he received it. "I thank your majesty." He took the crown to his monarch.

King Sennacherib rotated the crown in his fingers as he inspected the long purple gemstones. His eyes bulged and he shouted aggressively at his interpreter. A fervid exchange ensued which made Ella feel increasingly uncomfortable.

"What is the name of the adventurer who found these jewels?"

"Ronwind Drake, and he is the finest adventurer in the land."

The man's eyebrows rose, as though he knew who Ronwind Drake was. King Sennacherib seemed to swear, apparently also familiar with the name despite not speaking the language. Ella swallowed nervously, shrinking in her throne.

"We know of the one called Ronwind Drake, for he is a pirate, a thief and a scoundrel. He and his men ambushed one of our caravans, capturing four treasure chests, and later plundered one of our ships, stealing three more."

Ella looked horrified. "That's impossible! Ronwind is no pirate! You must have the wrong person."

The Assyrian continued, "He revealed his name to us while boasting that he was the greatest pirate on the seas! That surely tells you enough about what sort of a man he is. Those purple gems in your crown come from our mines."

The Queen shook her head. "No, it must be someone with a similar name. Ronwind found those treasures in an empty land."

"What empty land has jewels cut like these? These are among the rarest and most precious in the world. That is how His Eminence immediately recognised them. He could identify them by their very particular shape."

Ella thought about it. This man claimed that seven chests had been stolen, which was the same number that Ronwind had found, but Ella certainly trusted her Royal Adventurer more than she did these odd-looking people. There was surely a coincidence, a mistake or a misunderstanding of some kind going on, or they might simply be jealous of her crown and were outright lying.

The strange troupe conversed among themselves, which Queen Ella found rather rude, and she began to wonder if she would get her crown back. But it would be extremely foolhardy for the King of Assyria to cause any trouble at the World Fayre, miles from his home and before other leaders.

The rotund sovereign eventually handed the crown to his interpreter, who returned it to Ella. She nodded slightly and placed it back on her head.

"King Sennacherib has declared that you must return the stolen treasures within one month. That is, all of the gold, the silver and the jewels." The interpreter looked down and said nothing more. The blue-and-yellow procession turned, and the fish-wearing man's sapphire staff made that same strange sound as the parade exited the purple pavilion.

Ella stared incredulously at their backs, amazed by the arrogance she had just witnessed. She took off her crown and looked at those beautiful purple gemstones. Could Ronwind really have stolen them? It seemed unlikely. In any case, she had little time to dwell on the matter, because a great spectacle was about to occur outside, involving none other than the 'pirate' himself.

CHAPTER 8 – EMPIRE OF THE CLOUDS

A clamorous gathering surrounded a circular clearing at the World Fayre. In the middle of it, on a tall platform, stood a truly extraordinary contraption. Two huge sails flanked a log cabin, above which floated a canvas balloon supplied by hot air from a flame. Behind the ship trailed a triangular tail and a fluttering crescent. The sails were supported by wooden masts which could be turned from inside the cabin and a network of cords made them highly adjustable. Several thick ropes were connected to gigantic pegs in the ground to keep the tottering vessel from flying away.

This monstrous creation was the work of the realm's finest engineer, Astronaemius. The thin, red-robed man stood on the platform next to Ronwind Drake, who was dressed like a nobleman with a sword slung at his side. Between them, they would operate the mechanisms required to take the ship to the clouds.

Ronwind posed self-assuredly with hands on hips as he puffed his small chest out. "I am known as a great sailor," he shouted to the crowds below, "but today I become a winged conqueror! I leave as a sea lion but shall return as a golden eagle!" He held up a purple flag. "And when I reach that celestial realm, I will claim it for Her Majesty Queen Ella, so that she may also become Empress of the Clouds!"

There were cheers as the short adventurer waved the flag around. The two pioneers turned to enter the rectangular cabin and a door closed behind them. Workers began the process of detaching the ropes while the vessel teetered in the wind, seeming ready to burst into the skies. Giant ripples coursed through the vast expanses of canvas. The sheer immensity of this beast was terrifying. It was like seeing a colossal griffin chained down and desperately struggling to break free.

A member of the audience spoke, a scarlet cape flowing behind him as he came to the fore of one side of the clearing. "There is no realm in the sky," said Gaius Romulus Caesar. "There are only birds, and air."

"What of the heavens?" a bearded man chipped in from a different section of the crowd. Those around him nodded and murmured their agreement. "Just because you have not seen it, oh Caesar, does not mean that it does not exist."

One of Caesar's aides responded, "If such a realm existed, Caesar would have conquered it already!"

But Caesar put his hand up and his aide fell silent. "My empire is the candlelight in a pit of darkness. It is a realm of knowledge in a world of ignorance, and a legion of order in a sea of chaos. The most learned scholars, the wisest men and the best sages are all Praetorian. If there was any 'empire of the clouds', I would know about it and be the ruler of it. For all other nations lie in the shade of the great tree that is my civilization."

A silence fell upon the gathering. The men behind Caesar started to clap, slowly at first but rapidly breaking into a rapturous applause. The company parted and the scarlet emperor stepped back in among them.

The last rope was cut and the magnificent vessel lifted off, rising buoyantly as the side sails seemed to flap like the wings of a bird. Whether that was done for show or was a necessary mechanism, the crowd were overawed. The ship flew in a curved line and eventually disappeared over the hills.

The flock of spectators cried out in wonderment. Even some Praetorians clapped, impressed by the ingenuity of the invention if unconvinced by the veracity of its objective. King Sennacherib was heard to curse loudly. He had arrived too late and missed the opportunity to confront his nemesis, Ronwind Drake. The little 'pirate' was now on his way to plunder the treasures in the clouds.

In the same clearing from which the airship departed, an orchestra assembled. The Bard Laureate Gullivander conducted a rousing rendition of the Ode to Celtia, and the festivities for the rulers of the world then began in earnest. Throughout the day, sovereigns, aides and diplomats conversed. New trade deals were negotiated, treaties signed and ties strengthened. Ella felt proud that her event seemed to be bringing global rivals closer together, but she knew that words meant less than actions. Those of a cynical nature whispered that the emperors had only come here to establish whether this realm was worth invading.

King Bosgald of Borra spent much of his time trying to woo those alluring Veraskan women present throughout the fayre. Some were amused and led him on, but most ignored his advances and proceeded with their duties of patrolling and protecting dignitaries.

A continuous buffet banquet in the long feast tent provided food and drink at all hours. The delicacies on offer were enough to pacify the gluttonous King Sennacherib, who was a constant presence there while everyone else passed in and out. After the fat sovereign had consumed most of the lobster available, he and his Assyrian entourage decided to leave rather than stay for the remaining two days. They felt that it would be inappropriate to enjoy too much of Queen Ella's hospitality after having delivered her an ultimatum.

As darkness descended across the great plain at the end of the first day of the World Fayre, most of the rulers retired to their personal tents while a few stayed out to chat in the cool dusk air. Ella invited Gullivander to the garden of her paradisiacal purple pavilion because she needed some relaxing music after a stressful day. She reclined against an oak tree as white doves fluttered about above. The bard played on his lute and sung enchantingly.

"She rides upon a cloud,
Very vividly it glows,
That white celestial shroud,
Elegantly Ella goes,
Soaring above the crowd,
And only heaven knows,
How many have vowed,
To win the world rose."

Not for the first time, Gullivander found that his dreamy melodies had actually put Ella in dreamland. When he finished strumming those tender chords, the dainty monarch appeared to be asleep, so the bard left her and returned to his tent. Ella eventually moved to her more comfortable bedroom to get a good night's sleep.

On the morning of the second day of the World Fayre, a jovial sparring competition would be held which only sovereigns could enter. A circular arena had been built for the purpose and the rules were simple. Each competitor had a wooden sword and shield, and to touch your opponent's chest with your sword scored one point. The first to three points would win the duel. Queen Ella was adjudicator and sat upon a throne in the front row with Duncan at her side.

Eight rulers entered, some of whom were looking for a bit of fun and some of whom were aiming to win the tournament. The first match pitted Queen Nicola against Queen Bethan. Neither of these women had lifted a shield before, so it was not much of a duel. But many in the audience found the spectacle of two thinly-clad queens prancing around and giggling quite appealing. Nicola won the match by three points to two and proceeded to the semi-finals, which would probably be the furthest extent of her progress.

The second match of the first round saw King Bosgald come up against Margrave Melton. It was a one-sided encounter as the 'barbarian king' was much too powerful and explosive for the podgy margrave. Then Gaius Romulus Caesar faced Duchess Brady. The athletic emperor had a far longer reach than the petite ginger duchess, and he played to the crowd while toying with her, allowing her one token point on his way to the semi-finals.

The last match of the first round would be Viscount Elgar versus Duke Laurent. This seemed likely to be another unequal battle, as the grey-haired viscount limped into the arena to face the young duke. But when it started, the moustached old man displayed a surprising fastness of feet. Dancing about the arena, he immediately went on the offensive, feinting and bobbing to bamboozle his opponent. Elgar speedily scored a point with a swift jab to Laurent's chest. It was not clear how athletic the dark-haired duke was, as he wore baggy garments, but the viscount's tight leather garb revealed a wiry frame and supple upper body.

Finally Duke Laurent seemed to get going as he moved around more urgently on his toes. Elgar relaxed for a moment and Laurent spotted an opening, so lunged with his sword, but the wily old fox simply spun away. Suddenly Elgar sprung from the ground and struck Laurent's chest with a devastating counter-thrust. The duke appeared stunned, breathing heavily at two-nil down while the elderly man had yet to break sweat. Laurent charged again but this time Elgar blocked sword with shield.

"Come on!" the moustached maestro taunted as he skipped around confidently. The polite gentleman had turned into a rumbustious ruffian. He rapidly surged at the duke, twisting and probing as Laurent flailed his arms to try to keep up with his opponent rather than predict where he was about to go. The daring attack succeeded as Elgar's sword-tip found Laurent's front, touching him ever so slightly as though he did not require force.

The young duke felt humiliated, and so he should, for he had lost three-nil against a man three decades his elder. But Elgar consoled him and informed him that he had been a keen fencer since his youth. The embarrassment gave Duke Laurent a newfound determination to spend less time scoffing pastries in his chateau.

The first of the semi-finals saw Queen Nicola come up against King Bosgald. There would be no surprises in this one as the 'barbarian king' used his height and size to effortlessly attain three points. Bosgald was now the favourite to win the competition, because of his physique and clear prowess, but he had yet to be tested.

In the second semi-final, Viscount Elgar faced Gaius Romulus Caesar. It looked set to be an interesting encounter between two proficient duellists. They were similar in height, both naturally athletic, supple yet broad-shouldered men. Caesar had youth on his side, but Elgar had already shown that to count for little.

Queen Ella signalled for the match to start and Viscount Elgar instantly went on the offensive. His footwork was dazzling and his curved grey moustache bounced as he hopped about. Everything the old man did, he seemed to do with a certain veneer. Sharp and evasive, he demonstrated an attacking finesse which betrayed his years. He quickly found an opening and the crowd cheered as Elgar gained the first point against a seemingly bewildered Praetorian Emperor.

But Caesar was a fast learner and he would not fall for the cunning dog's feints again. He upped his game and began to show an impressive level of nimbleness himself, dodging and diving to unsettle his opponent. Caesar seemed to know what was coming and Elgar jabbed at the emperor's scarlet cape as it billowed in the space where he had once been. The Praetorian noticed that the flamboyant gentleman had little concept of defence, rarely bringing his shield up when he charged, so Caesar delivered a series of subtle counter-attacks to score two points in quick succession.

The moustached maestro appeared startled but he was not finished yet. A truly epic duel ensued as Elgar stormed forward, this time using his shield to parry Caesar's deft thrusts. Elgar ducked, feinted, coiled and sprang, and spectators clamoured as his sword drove inevitably towards Caesar's chest for a certain point.

But the scarlet emperor brought his shield up at lightning speed and somehow deflected the viscount's weapon. The crowd gasped and Elgar himself appeared so astonished that he let his guard down for a couple of seconds. Caesar jabbed promptly to take the point and the match.

"Well done," Elgar said as he vigorously shook Caesar's hand. "That contest both thrilled and delighted me." Caesar smiled and congratulated the skilful viscount on his efforts while the audience gave him a standing ovation. Elgar received a kiss from Queen Ella as he went into the stands to watch the final.

After a short break, the two finalists entered the circular floor of the brimming arena. Ella hoped that the challengers would not take it too seriously, since it was just a jovial sparring competition, but both men seemed very determined to win and thereby impress the watching maiden.

The burly King Bosgald was a couple of inches taller than Gaius Romulus Caesar, but Caesar seemed more graceful. Though the clean-shaven emperor was considerably thinner than the bearded monarch, he had a powerful chest and refined muscularity. Both of them wore light armour and a cape, one of auburn and one of scarlet. Spectators whispered amongst themselves as they tried to predict the outcome of the fight, but there was no clear favourite. The two appeared roughly equal in prowess as well as in popularity.

Queen Ella raised her staff to signify the beginning of the contest. Bosgald moved forward slowly with his shield raised but Caesar left his down and backed away. The larger man glimpsed an early opportunity and thrust forcefully with his wooden sword, but in a stunning display of dexterity, the emperor simply side-stepped. It was an audacious dodge, arrogant even, and the crowd roared their approval.

King Bosgald appeared annoyed and charged more vigorously, but Caesar swerved the other way. It was like watching a bull and a matador. The scarlet matador was always one step ahead of the raging bull. After turning with remarkable swiftness again, Caesar's sword neatly touched his rival's chest and the stadium erupted. It was the first serious point that the mighty King Bosgald had conceded. Even Queen Ella, who had mostly been unmoved by the contests, gasped and edged forward on her seat.

Bosgald suddenly went berserk, allowing Caesar no time to celebrate his point. The hefty warrior's auburn cape waved behind him as he went shield-first with the aim of shunting his enemy.

Caesar blocked using his buffer, stumbling back but managing to maintain his composure.

The barbarian king snarled like a frenzied beast. When he rushed forth again, the scarlet emperor ducked low to trip the bearded aggressor. Bosgald fell flat on his face and dropped his items. He desperately scrambled for his shield, but the tip of Caesar's sword was already upon his torso.

"That isn't fair! He tripped me!" King Bosgald looked pleadingly at Queen Ella.

"You charged at him," Ella replied, "which gave him the opportunity to trip you, and the rules do not forbid any such action. But please try not to upset your opponent, Caesar."

The Praetorian grinned and Bosgald grumbled before dusting himself off and picking up his pieces. He glowered at Caesar but did not move this time, apparently realising that his aggression was not reaping rewards. King Bosgald waited for Caesar to attack and the crowd enthusiastically encouraged the scarlet emperor to finish the duel. Caesar had been on the defensive for most of the match, letting his opponent lead which had allowed him to repeatedly counter. The onus was now on him to spar offensively and show why he was worthy of victory.

Caesar lurched forward, only to pull back rapidly, as he sought to open up his rival, but Bosgald was having none of it. The raging bull had become a stubborn bulldog, holding his shield in front of him, and spectators began to boo the stagnating duel.

Suddenly the barbarian king sprung into action as he surged at his adversary once more. This time, he brought up his sword to slash at Caesar's face. The scarlet emperor did not turn his head quickly enough and the surprise blow stunned him. Bosgald knocked Caesar's sword and shield away before thrusting at the unarmed man's chest. Caesar tumbled backwards and Bosgald scored his first point.

The emperor lay on the ground in a daze as his cheek bled. Ella gaped at the scene, disgusted by what her friendly competition had turned into. King Bosgald held his arms aloft as his supporters cheered him, but in reality he was no longer sparring; he was assaulting his opponent. Ella was uncertain whether she should intervene, for stopping these men might enrage them further, and she was keen to have good relations with both. The crowd seemed to be enjoying the vigorous contest and Ella did not want to look like a spoilsport by calling a premature end to proceedings.

Then a fawn bulldog leapt from the audience and scampered along the arena floor. Duncan lunged for the sword on the ground and snatched it in his teeth.

"Hey," said Bosgald, "don't ruin the fight now, doggy." He held out a hand. "Give us that sword."

But the bulldog evaded him playfully, seeming to think that this was a game. He had watched the men fighting and now he wanted to be part of the action. Duncan snarled and clamped his powerful jaw on the wooden weapon. A crunching sound was heard as it snapped in two, one end drooping out of the mutt's mouth.

"That's my sword!" Caesar complained.

Ella struggled to contain the grin playing on her lips. "Oh Duncan! You silly little dog! How can we continue the duel now?" The Queen got off her throne. "Sorry boys, this competition is over."

The bulldog lowered his head as he chewed on wood. Ella walked over to Duncan and patted him while the dumbfounded duellists looked at each other.

The Praetorian protested, "I was winning, so let me be declared the victor."

Bosgald laughed. "You were on your backside, Caesar, and you're bleeding."

Caesar muttered and put a hand to the side of his face, where he felt blood. Bosgald's violent slash had cut a small opening on the skin, which had painted the scarlet emperor's cheek red.

"Well," said Queen Ella, "neither of you have won, so I shall declare Duncan to be the winner."

The bulldog seemed to gaze up proudly as his long tongue flailed. Ella congratulated the men on their efforts and suggested that they shake hands. They did so grudgingly, and the crowd clapped as the contestants left to go and get cleaned up.

CHAPTER 9 – A GROSS FLARE

The main theatrical event of the World Fayre would be a grandiose musical play entitled *The Lily of the Valley*. The 'floral tragicomedy' was written and directed by the Bard Laureate Gullivander, but little had been revealed, so there was much excitement. Before a wooden stage, crowds gathered on benches. Queen Ella and her bulldog had prime seats.

Purple curtains opened to reveal a fantastical wild scene. Upon the stage was an assortment of giant flowers, plants, mushrooms and other flora. It was evidently an enlarged setting intended to make the actors look pint-sized. In the middle was a red orchid, on the right was a willow tree and on the left was a waterfall running into a pond. The stage had no rear wall so hills in the distance provided the background.

An actress dressed as a flower appeared from the thickets and spun around the orchid. Six pink petals drooped from her head and pointed leaves hung from her frock. While Gullivander's orchestra played a delicate, airy tune, the Lily twirled on her feet and declared, "I am the princess Lily of the Valley, and today I become queen."

A line of green-garbed children came out and chanted an ode as they spiralled around the Lily. A branch fell from above, which the Lily caught, making it her royal staff. The little people passed white flowers along their line as they prepared a headpiece for their new monarch. When it was complete, the crown of daisies was tossed into the air, and the Lily leapt like a ballerina to catch it upon her head. Now the coronation of Queen Lily of the Valley was complete, and the green subjects filed off stage. A merry tune followed as a young man dressed as a seed appeared and started to sing.

"Bonny Queen Lily,
I am the Poplar Prince,
You may call me silly,
But I come here to convince.
I saw you, Queen Lily,
By the tree of golden quince,
You looked so fair and frilly,
And I have loved you ever since."
The Lily stared at the seed rather angrily and chastised him.

"You silly poplar seed,
Do not spoil my day,
You know I give no heed,
To anything you say,
I would rather hear a weed,
Than listen to you neigh,
So please now do a deed,
And from me go away!"

Queen Lily flailed her arms and shook her fists to repel the Poplar Prince, who protected himself and started to sob before singing again.

"Won't you listen to my plea,
There is no need to shove,
Though I am lower than a bee,
I shall be higher than a dove,
For I want to make you see,
My fair and dainty love,
That when I am a poplar tree,
I will reach the skies above."

Suddenly a short, bearded figure crashed down onto the stage from the willow tree. He stood up and began to bellow.

"I am the Wizard of the Willow,
But I tumbled from my tree,
For winds up there do billow,
And now down here you see me."

Queen Lily turned her attention to the wizard.

"Oh you most annoying thing,
If you are truly wise,
Then listen to me sing,
For I am sick of hearing lies,
Magic you will bring,
I shall close my eyes,
And then my handsome king,
Before me he must rise."

The Wizard of the Willow spun around and uttered his reply.

"You silly foolish queen,
You know not what you ask,
But since you are so mean,
I will do this woeful task."

He held his arms aloft and cast a spell on the Lily.

"So then you shall sleep,
And not to be revived,
In a slumber of the deep,
Until your king has arrived."

The Lily collapsed on the floor amid dramatic music. The Wizard of the Willow vanished and the Poplar Prince tried unsuccessfully to rouse the Queen. The little green people returned and attempted to wake their sleeping monarch but to no avail. They lamented the tragic situation and lifted her onto a bed of moss so that she would be more comfortable. An entirely blue figure then emerged from behind the pond and broke into song.

"I am the Prince of the Pond,
I will rouse the dreaming daughter,
For we share such a bond,
I shall wake her with my water!"

He splashed water from his pond in the direction of the slumbering maiden, and a delicate staccato piece played while Queen Lily was pattered by droplets, but she did not flinch. Suddenly, brilliant string music began as a rotund man wearing a magnificent gold mask entered.

"I am the glorious Sun King,
The one who dazzles up high,
I radiate over everything,
I am that beacon of the sky,
I will wake the Lily Queen,
With my gaze most bright,
My rays so hot and keen,
She shall see my burning light."

A brazier was lit and the stage became brighter. The Prince of the Pond stepped forward to confront the Sun King.

"Why would she want you,
Illuminator of the Earth,
I doubt you ever knew,
A valley of such little worth,
You cannot show her care,
Nor the love that she needs,
For you are a gross flare,
And we live among the weeds."

The Sun King threateningly bore down on the Prince of the Pond.
"I would advise you stop,
For I could dry up your lake,
Evaporate every drop,
All your water I can take."
Just as the Prince of the Pond was about to respond, a tall figure in a black-and-white feathered suit leapt onto the stage. He had a dark beak and twirled to display purplish-blue wings. "I am the Marvellous Master Magpie, and the maiden will be mine!" A zesty and melodramatic score played.
"I am the master of every bird,
Every sparrow, starling, quail,
Surely you have heard,
Our chirping in the vale."
As he hopped around the bemused pair, the Sun King folded his arms and the Prince of the Pond protested.
"I doubt you are their chief,
For a magpie is a crook,
A trickster and a thief,
Hardly different to a rook,
You dazzle with your plume,
But you are really just a crow,
Those harbingers of doom,
You are every bit as low!"
The Marvellous Master Magpie spun away and sung again.
"I will awaken the girl,
With our stirring sound,
A great symphonic swirl,
To raise her from the ground."
The magpie lifted his wings, a door on the stage floor opened and a flock of birds flew out. The audience gasped as a spectacular variety of feathered creatures spiralled around the magpie, seeming to prove that he truly was the master of all the birds in the valley.
But some of them crashed into things and fell, and the actors had to shield themselves from the mass of beating wings and beaks. One onlooker took a particular disliking to this squawking frenzy. Ella was so engrossed in the play that she was not watching her pet bulldog. Duncan leapt onto the stage and bounded boldly into the middle of the flock, creating even more hysteria among them.

The Sun King managed to grab the canine's red leash, and held it as Duncan pulled back. "No!" Ella called. "Stop! It will slip off!" As the bulldog reversed, his collar indeed began to slip over his head. Characteristic of the stout breed, Duncan's powerful neck was as thick as his noggin, and he was quite capable of escaping his restraints if persistent enough.

But the Sun King held firm, apparently not hearing Ella among the screeching swarm. The collar popped off Duncan's head and suddenly the fawn bulldog was free. His eyes glinted manically and his tongue dangled out as he pranced around, lunging at those poor avian creatures who were unable to flee the congested stage. They frantically fluttered and squawked while the bulldog snarled and swiped in the midst of the maelstrom. Starlings and sparrows tumbled, sprawling across the floor.

"We'll never get that collar back on now!" Ella shouted. "He needs to be calm first!" The Queen tried calling her bulldog, but he was far too excited to obey or even notice his mistress. Careering around the floral scenery, the stocky dog knocked over props and snapped his jaw at any actor who tried to grab him. It was enough to wake the Lily from her slumber. The dainty maiden cut a bitter, haggard figure as she moaned, "Someone has to stop this mutt!"

Duncan was not a vicious dog, just excessively playful, and had a tendency to get out of control once he reached a level of excitement. Fortunately, one member of the backstage team came up with the clever idea of getting a long rope and tying a loop which could be thrown like a lasso. While Duncan ran amok, the noose landed over his head, and the man holding the rope stayed behind the misbehaving bulldog so that he could not pull free. Duncan panted loudly, subdued and soon accepted his fate as a collared mutt again. The remaining birds escaped the stage while the crew member led Duncan away and he trotted off obediently.

But suddenly two more starlings appeared from the sub-chamber and flapped their wings while chittering harshly, which enraged Duncan. The bulldog turned sharply and charged at the birds. So powerful and abrupt was his burst that the man holding the rope fell over at the edge of the stage while desperately clinging on.

Duncan strained like a bull, determined to catch a bird after all of his failed attempts, and the frayed end of the rope slipped free from the fallen fellow's fingers. The resultant shift in momentum caused the bulldog to tumble forward and he collided with the brazier at the back of the stage, which crashed to the floor and spilled its blazing contents.

A large flame shot up as actors and spectators screamed. Luckily, the scalding oils had not hit any person or animal, but the fire would spread quickly. Duncan looked terrified and sprinted to the other side of the stage. The rope that trailed behind the bulldog snagged on a burning bush, which dragged along and gathered other props in its path. Duncan bounded into fields beyond the stage while a giant flaming mushroom bumped along the ground behind him. The bulldog, completely oblivious to the chaos he had caused, was now focussed on escaping from the fiery menace which seemed to be chasing him through the grass.

There was nothing that anyone could do to stop the fire. The actors fled and the audience evacuated as fumes billowed towards them. Gullivander remained in the front row, staring at months of his artistic work as it disappeared amid a great blaze; that beautiful, crafted scenery consumed by a vast, glowing haze. Not for the first time, an event had been ruined by a frisky fawn bulldog.

From a rear bench, a moustached old man stood up and clapped enthusiastically. "What an enthralling spectacle!" Viscount Elgar declared, unaware that this grand disaster was not part of the show. He started to cough and splutter as the smoke swirled around him, and hobbled away.

Next to the stage was a big tent, which also caught fire, and those inside it scarpered. Ella watched from a distance, flailing her arms and screaming for someone to do something. Staff with barrels rushed to the edge of the fire and hurled water, but such a large and aggressive inferno could not be extinguished. Towering flames crept along the top of the tent and it began to crumple like paper. Nearby were tables, chairs, crates and more canvas which would soon be ablaze.

The increasingly intense heat of the uncontainable fire made it unapproachable. Veraskan guardswomen ordered everyone to collect their belongings and leave the World Fayre. Gaius Romulus Caesar, King Bosgald, Queen Nicola and the rest gathered their parties, and as many of their items as they could safely acquire, and left the great plain.

Ella suddenly thought of Duncan and ran to the large field behind the stage. She saw her bulldog frolicking among daisies in a tranquil meadow. Duncan caught sight of his mistress and bounded eagerly towards her, tongue flailing and jowls slapping against his chin. Snorting through his nose, Duncan playfully jumped up at Ella, but she did not look happy. The boisterous bulldog was blissfully unaware that he was the root source of the colossal catastrophe.

Ella led Duncan out of the field and they exited through a gate in the palisade wall. The Queen and the bulldog walked up a wooded hillside and gazed over the flaming disaster. Ella sat on a log and Duncan looked up at her with his big brown eyes. He sniffled, sensing that she was annoyed with him, but he did not know why. The bulldog licked at her ankles, which would normally get a reaction, but Ella was silent.

After half an hour of tearful contemplation, the Queen regarded her pet. "Well, you managed to wake the Queen Lily, so you must be the one for her." She cuddled her canine companion as they watched the great fire in the plain before them. In the middle of it was that huge purple pavilion and a smile was raised on Ella's lips that her tent still stood.

But the gold sphere at its apex began to sink as flames crept up and then the whole thing folded. Released above it were many fabrics of purple, pink and red, which swirled around like the clothes of an exotic dancer. Ella and Duncan stayed on the hill for the rest of the day and night, kept warm by the inferno.

*

Sat upon her throne in the onyx hall, the Queen was in a state. Unlike her, her hair was unkempt and she wore a simple brown dress which did not even fit. Ella summoned her Lord Treasurer.

"Quintus, my whole realm is collapsing!" the bedraggled monarch moaned.

"What? Nonsense, my majesty! Although the World Fayre ended in catastrophe, it was a success for two days. And many of the sovereigns were due to leave that night anyway."

"Well, it's not just that. At the fayre, I met the King of Assyria. He looked at my crown and declared that the purple jewels on it are his! He said that Ronwind Drake is a pirate who stole seven treasure chests from his empire, and he demanded that we return everything within one month!"

Quintus placed a hand on his mouth, taking a while to answer.

"Perhaps he was mistaken. I trust good Ronwind more than I do the King of Assyria, wherever that is!"

Ella frowned. "But they knew the name of Ronwind Drake. As soon as I spoke it, they gasped, and seemed sure that he is a pirate!"

The Lord Treasurer stroked his brown beard. "Perhaps they were bluffing, your majesty. Perhaps they were going to gasp at any name. How would they even know the name of the person who plundered them?"

Queen Ella tilted her head. "They said that Ronwind proclaimed himself as the greatest pirate on the high seas!"

Quintus scoffed and waved a hand. "Why would you give your name to someone that you have robbed? Ronwind is no fool, nor is he a thief. He is a decent man who would never commit such a foul and idiotic act."

Ella stared in thought at the fountain ahead. She seemed to be coming round to Quintus's arguments but still had her doubts. "Their king looked most angry, shouting and pointing, which would be hard to fake if it was a con."

The Lord Treasurer shrugged. "Either he was acting or he was mistaken... Which leads to the question of how one can possibly be sure that a gemstone is theirs? Moreover, is the Assyrian Empire not thousands of miles away? If you ignore his ultimatum, what can he actually do? I am certain that nothing will come of this except perhaps more angry words from an emissary."

The Queen's shoulders relaxed and she began to look less tense. Quintus continued, "I'd say that it was an elaborate con. Their king probably had a fit of envy when he saw your wonderful crown, so he tried to trick your majesty out of your treasures."

"They were a strange lot," Ella remarked. "One of them wore a fish upon his head."

Quintus laughed. "They sound like a bunch of crooks to me. I wonder if that man was even the King of Assyria? They have well and truly played you for the fool, my dear majesty."

Ella glared at Quintus, seeming to be offended by that comment. The bearded officer hastily added, "It is because you are a trusting person, your highness. They sensed it; your kindness, your honour, your pureness even. Those scoundrels sought to exploit our fair monarch."

The Queen gazed out the window, sighing as she reclined in her throne. "You are right, Quintus. I am too lovely for my own good sometimes. People try to take advantage."

"That's precisely it."

"So you think I should just ignore them?"

"Of course," Quintus said. "It would be impossible to return those treasures anyway. We have already distributed much of the gold and silver to the poor people of this realm, and one of the chests went missing."

Ella nodded. "I am glad that I have you to talk to, Quintus. You are good at keeping me down to earth. Not only do I trust people too much, but sometimes I worry too much, and with all of my duties, I let everything get on top of me."

"It is because you care, your majesty, as a compassionate individual who has a deep affinity with your populace. You work so very hard for them, too hard perhaps. That is your only sin."

"Thank you." The Queen waved her hand to dismiss the Lord Treasurer, who bowed before leaving.

Ella's mail was brought before her. It mostly seemed to consist of routine correspondence, which could be dealt with by her staff, but one letter caught her eye. On the front of a red envelope, Ella's name was encapsulated by a heart. She tore it open and saw a picture of a rose with some words nearby.

"Rose of the World,

I will wait for you for Eternity,

For Eternity is in you."

Ella's big blue eyes scanned the anonymous love letter, unsure if she was flattered or perturbed. She reached into her pocket and pulled out her rose key, that red porcelain flower with gold metal twisted around its green stem. As she twirled the ornamental object in her fingers, Ella pondered who might have written the note, but came to the conclusion that there were too many possibilities.

CHAPTER 10 – STORM IN A TEACUP

The Queen had recently decided that she would embark on a national tour. One of the purposes of the World Fayre had been to bring the people of her realm together, but that event had ended in disaster, so now Ella would go to her people. The commoners of Celtia had enjoyed the carnival but Ella was worried that her reputation had been damaged. The purple monarch planned to visit every settlement in her nation and win over the hearts of her subjects. It was also an opportunity to perform a great survey of the realm, for the Lord Treasurer had long been keen to compile a 'Domesday Book' of sorts; a record of each citizen's holdings in land and livestock.

Ella and Quintus were escorted by two dozen Veraskan guards. They were also accompanied by the Bard Laureate Gullivander, whose ensemble's music would amplify the enchanting effect that royalty had on people. For once, Duncan was left at home, because he could not be trusted after recent escapades.

The first settlement which the regal party came across was Doff, a small village surrounded by woodlands near the Tundra Castle. The three carriages pulled up and the folk came out of their stone dwellings, bowing and saying words of grace. But one villager did not act so courteously. A scrawny, scruffy man jabbed his finger at the Queen and shouted, "She is not the rightful monarch!"

Ella quizzically regarded the rude chap, who seemed to resemble a human rodent and wore grey rags with a brown headscarf. He moved towards the Queen but the Veraskan women blocked his path with their shields.

"Let him pass," Ella said, and the guards parted. "If I am not the rightful monarch, then who is?"

"I am!"

The villagers laughed at the filthy pretender. "He is only the king fool."

Two Veraskans grabbed the rascal but Ella raised a hand. "Wait. I wish to hear him out. Why would you say that you are the monarch?"

"Because the Tenth Zai states so."

"The who?" Ella narrowed her eyes.

"Not the who, but the what. Surely you have heard of the Zais?"

Queen Ella glanced at Quintus, who appeared as confused as her, and a commoner spoke up. "Please your majesty, ignore him. We all do. He is the village idiot."

But Ella seemed intrigued and kept her attention on the odd fellow. "What are these 'Zais' then?"

He produced a book from his satchel entitled *Compendium of Zais*. "I will begin with the First Zai. *Introspective Conversation With The World Serpent*."

"What?" Quintus said, but the man simply adjusted his headscarf and began.

"Do you intend on rising from your pit to rule the world once more?" He clicked his fingers. "Yes," he replied to himself.

"Hath you wrath that you stuff the trough of froth with mirth?" he asked and clicked his fingers again. "No." He tapped his foot.

"And will you thrill the chill of my still quill by inking it? No," he said and tapped his foot again.

"Does this Zai end here?" He clicked his fingers. "Yes."

There was silence all around. Ella's face was a picture of bewilderment, her lips pursed in a circle and one eyebrow raised. Quintus stared speechlessly at the strange performer, who then looked up. "What do you think?"

"Um," Queen Ella said, "it's rather… spiffy."

"Then I shall perform the Second Zai," and without further ado he began. "*Eternal Echo Of The Sewer King*."

"He doth wander alone in the endless tunnels of his internal, infernal sewage pot.

He doth cry when the rats rot and the pigeons perish, for he is all alone.

He doth question this Zai.

Yet I silently sidestep He Who Is Most Rattish.

I weep. He calls.

I weep yet further. He calls yet further.

He calls, he calls, HE CALLS.

ECHO, ECHO."

The rat-like man writhed in circular motions as his lengthy fingernails clung to his headscarf.

"ECHO, ECHO," he repeated, before quietening. He breathed heavily, soaked in sweat, and looked down.

Ella's mouth hung open as she observed the peculiar scene. Even the usually immovable Veraskans appeared disturbed by the spectacle. The little man regained his composure. "Would you like to hear the next one?"

Ella nodded faintly and Quintus rolled his eyes.

"The Third Zai, *Red Nell*," the performer announced.

"Red Ned bled,
Dead bloodshed,
Ned's ruddy Nell,
Is redder than hell,
But who is Ned,
And what is Nell,
You cry out in query and quell,
Ned is the redhead,
And Red Nell is thee,
But how can that be?
For I thought that Red Nell was me."

Quintus stepped forward. "Can we put a stop to this utter drivel, your majesty? I cannot stand it any longer."

Ella looked at the eccentric individual. "Did you write these Zais?"

"Yes."

"Well, you aren't going to be the King of Celtia any time soon, despite what the Tenth Zai might say, but there may be a place for you in my society yet. I believe that you show considerable potential as a poetic performer, and I can offer to put you under the tutorage of my Bard Laureate, Master Gullivander."

The scrawny man appeared humbled. His arrogant demeanour altered and he gratefully accepted the invitation of a bardic scholarship. The people of Doff were impressed by their Queen, for she had ridden them of a nuisance and given the misfit a purpose in life. The royal carriages were cheered as they departed the village.

Taversham was the next settlement that they came across. This important trade centre stood on the intersection between two major roads in the heartland of Celtia. Its market was among the largest in the country and much of the produce came from the extensive farms surrounding the town.

Gullivander's marching band led the parade and mounted Veraskan guards rode on all sides as they passed cottages and cornfields on the east fringe of Taversham. It was a scorching day and dust from the earth seemed to hang in the air.

The Queen's entourage were greeted by some fanatical folk but the place seemed surprisingly empty. As the regal tourists moved towards the centre of town, they started to hear chanting and hollering.

Soon this noise was loud enough to drown out Gullivander's music, and it became apparent that a thunderous tumult was taking place in Taversham. This concentrated commotion did not sound like cheering, nor was it directed at the royal visitors. Ella looked through an avenue between buildings and caught a glimpse of the riot, which she ordered her carriages towards.

Wheels bumped along cobblestones and horses neighed in distress as they approached the tempest. When they halted, the Queen and the Lord Treasurer stepped onto the street, encircled by a layer of Verasakan guards. They moved up to the chaotic scenes.

The congregation of angry townsfolk surrounded a wood-and-brick warehouse. Some waved flaming pitchforks. How exactly they managed to set alight such implements was unclear, but it achieved the intended effect of intimidation.

When those at the back of the crowd realised that the monarch and her staff were among them, some fell silent and dropped to their knees, while others simply shouted their consternations. Ella was a bit taken aback, but they did not appear to be venting their anger at her. Rather, they seemed to be passionately trying to explain themselves.

"We are petitioning in strength and deed!" one declared.

"I hope the justices of the peace will take order that we poor men shall have corn without such violence," another remarked before being enveloped by the mob.

"I'd as leaffe losse my life as see my wife and children stearve!" a bearded fellow cried.

Since they were all clamouring over one another, the Queen found it difficult to discern exactly what the problem was. Ella saw one woman who looked relatively mild and measured among the mayhem, so she asked her to step within the Veraskan circle. The guards allowed her into their chain-like formation and the dark-haired women curtsied before the purple-clad monarch.

"Could you please explain what is going on here?"

"Humblest greetings to your highness. It is the greatest honour of my life. I shall do my best to explain what is happening in this fair town of your royal crown."

The Queen nodded as she held her staff in one hand and waved her other to gesture for the woman to continue.

"The people of Taversham are aggrieved by a badger."

Ella blinked and furrowed her brow. "A badger?"

"Indeed, your highness. That is what I have been told. This badger has been engrossing corn, and I believe it is currently hiding in that warehouse." She pointed at the sturdy barn which the townsfolk seemed to be threatening to burn down.

"I see." Ella looked at Quintus, who appeared equally perplexed. "Emerald," she said to her chief guard, "Disperse this mob and tell them that we shall sort it out." The Queen turned to the woman again. "What exactly do you mean by 'engrossing' corn?"

"Eating it, your highness, I presume."

"Right. How odd. Well, I won't have them burning down a warehouse for the sake of a corn-hungry badger."

Emerald's unit efficiently broke up the crowd using their shields and horses and they doused the flaming pitchforks. Within minutes, the mob was subdued and a path had been cleared to the warehouse.

First, they had to find a way in. The mob had been trying to bash the main door down but that looked like a hopeless task. Skilled Veraskan women went around the building and located a weak spot. They hacked away with their axes and soon created an opening.

Once the gap was sufficiently wide, the Queen and the Lord Treasurer were escorted in. They found themselves in a large room containing many scattered boxes. It was rather dark, so Emerald lit a torch. Some Veraskans remained outside to guard the entrance while Gullivander attempted to pacify the people with his music.

The red-haired figure of Emerald led the group through the clutter, when suddenly they saw a flash of mulberry on the far side of the room. "Hey!" the Veraskan shouted. "Stop and show yourself, in the name of the Queen!"

A tall man emerged from behind a crate. Two horns of purple hair wobbled as he approached with his hands up. "I've done nothing wrong!"

"Then why were you hiding behind those boxes?" Emerald questioned.

"I..." As he moved nearer, his gaze fell upon the Queen and he trailed off.

Ella looked at the distinctive man in the outlandish outfit and mulberry cape. Her eyes widened, for she knew who he was.

"Jandrole Heth!"

"Ella! You are... The Queen?" He remembered the young woman who had walked with him through the woods months ago.

"I am. How nice it is to see you again, but please tell me what you are doing here?"

"This is my warehouse," Jandrole said. "But right now I am hiding, for the townsfolk wish to kill me!"

"I thought they were looking for a badger?"

"I am that badger!"

The Queen gawked, and Quintus spoke, "Your majesty, I believe I know what the woman meant by an 'engrossing badger' now. It occurred to me that I studied these terms during my degree in economic law. A badger is a merchant who buys food in one place and sells it at another. 'Engrossing' refers to buying out the majority of that victual, which creates a monopoly and inevitably results in the rising of price. Along with regrating and forestalling, such an action artificially inflates market value. This, I surmise, is why the people of Taversham are angry. They have been priced out of their corn."

"Well," Ella said, "thank you for remembering that just now. What a useful advisor you are, Quintus. Does that mean Jandrole here has broken the law?"

The purple-haired merchant looked horrified. "I didn't know," he pleaded but Ella put a palm up to silence him.

Quintus stroked his long beard. "I would have to check the particular law. I am not very familiar with the ins and outs of it."

"Then here is what we shall do," said the Queen. "You will apologise to the people of Taversham, Jandrole, for your greediness. You will hand them all of your corn for free. I know that you can afford this, because you are a rich man who deals in a great variety of goods. I will pay for your warehouse to be repaired because my Veraskans hacked it open."

The merchant swallowed and nodded. Emerald and her women frog-marched Jandrole out of the warehouse, taking him to the town square, where he stood up on a platform and said sorry for his avaricious actions. He vowed to be a good merchant from now on and tossed many sacks of corn to the hungry masses.

The commoners made merry amid a great celebration of mead and corn cakes. Hence, Queen Ella had solved the tumult in Taversham and increased her popularity in another settlement of Celtia.

The following day, the touring party found themselves on an unusual track. Verged by dense woodland, vines arched across the top of the route, such that it was enclosed by nature. It was also a very long, straight road, and this corridor of foliage appeared to extend for infinity.

The royal carriages travelled along the serene, surreal route for an hour with no end in sight. Then on their left came a row of slender arborvitae trees with an opening in the middle. Queen Ella ordered her company to halt and they turned their heads to look down the perpendicular pathway. More tall trees lined this avenue and in the distance were two noticeable sights; a large multi-coloured mansion from which various crooked spires pointed and a giant blue-and-white teacup.

"What is that?" asked the Queen.

Her Lord Treasurer answered, "I believe that is the estate of Astronaemius, the great engineer, the one who sailed to the clouds with Ronwind, your majesty."

"Oh. Well, I'm sure someone will be around." The vehicles proceeded towards the curious estate.

They stopped before the multi-coloured mansion and a circular door opened. A medium-sized man, dressed in a dark suit and top hat, bent forward to hobble out of the doorway. He seemed quite startled as he looked at the congregation.

Queen Ella stepped out of her carriage. "Hello there. I understand that this is the estate of Astronaemius?"

"It is. But I am in charge of it while he is away."

"I see. And what is your name?"

"Idiom."

"Nice to meet you, Idiom. I suspect that you have already guessed who I am. We are touring my realm and surveying every holding. Do you mind if I take a look around?"

"Horses for courses," said Idiom.

Ella blinked. "Pardon?"

"Horses are for courses, not mansions."

"Oh. Well I was going to leave my horses here."

"Then do come in." Idiom held the door open, and Ella and Quintus entered. They stepped onto a slanted floor and leaned against the wall, which was also slanted. It seemed like the whole corridor had been twisted around. Idiom produced a red pointy hat, which he handed to Quintus. "Wear this."

"Why?"

"You'll find out later."

Quintus put on the rather silly-looking hat and Ella grinned. "You haven't heard anything from Astronaemius since he left?" inquired the Queen of the engineer's assistant.

Idiom shook his head. "No."

"I do hope that he and Ronwind return soon. I intend to hold a great ball in my castle to celebrate their achievements."

"Well, the ball's in your court." Idiom grasped his left arm with his right hand and a woody click was heard.

"You have a fake arm?" Ella said, suddenly realising that he had not moved his left arm yet.

"No need to add insult to injury. My leg is wooden too."

"What happened?"

"I bought a very expensive painting."

"And how did that result in your situation?"

"It cost me an arm and a leg. Never buy artwork. Just think about it instead."

The Queen's face screwed into an expression of puzzlement. "What do you mean?"

"A penny for your thoughts. Much cheaper. Now come along." Idiom hobbled down the warped corridor and they entered a musty chamber. "That's the painting." He pointed at a large picture on the wall.

The regal visitors looked at it, but all they could see were various metaphors and phrases scrawled in different colours and styles. "What sort of a painting is this?" Quintus asked. "I see only words."

"A picture paints a thousand words."

"Right." Quintus nodded. "What's it called?"

"Speak of the Devil."

"Why?"

"Because it's about the devil."

"I don't see anything about the devil."

"Look closer. The devil's in the detail."

Ella and Quintus studied the strange painting for a while and then sighed. Idiom handed Quintus a tattered book. "Try my novel instead."

"This book is missing its edges."

"To make a long story short, I cut corners. But never judge a book by its cover."

Quintus put the book down and looked at Ella as though to say 'Let's get out of here', but the Queen seemed quite amused. Idiom led his guests across the room and opened a metal door.

Outside again, the trio strolled along the estate's unkempt gardens, through which a river flowed. On the far side of the water was a huge china teacup. "That's amazing," said Ella. "Can we get a closer look?"

"Not yet," Idiom replied. "We're on the wrong side of the river."

"Well, there is a bridge over there." Ella pointed.

"We'll cross that bridge when we come to it. Hang on! Did you hear that?"

"No. What?"

"I heard something on the grapevine." Idiom walked past a molehill and stared up at a tree, from which a grapevine hung. "Look. A cat among the pigeons." Some grey birds flew away in panic. "Not to fear. My dog will sort it out. Hector!"

A white poodle came bounding along and proceeded to woof. "He's barking up the wrong tree," Idiom murmured before picking up a spade and starting to dig.

"What the heck are you doing?" asked Quintus.

"I'm making a mountain out of a molehill," said Idiom as soil flew from his spade towards the mound.

"Why?"

"Because it seems like a curious thing to do." Idiom shrugged and kept shovelling.

"How on earth will that help your predicament?" The red-hatted man put his hands on his hips.

"Curiosity killed the cat."

"What? You intend to kill the cat?" Quintus glanced towards Ella.

"Not exactly." Idiom picked up a bottle of white liquid and poured it on the heap of earth.

"Wait," Ella said. "Are you using milk to attract the cat, so that you can hurt it? I'm not happy with this."

"Don't cry over spilt milk."

The ginger cat leapt from the tree and dashed away. Idiom sighed. "I'll show you my chicken coop instead." He led them into a small barn. "Want some eggs?"

"Not especially," Quintus replied, adjusting his hat which had been knocked out of position by the low entrance.

"Go on." Idiom handed him a basket. "These eggs will be wasted otherwise. You can give them to your servants, or peasants in the next town that you visit."

"Very well." Quintus started to place eggs into the basket.

"Stop. Don't put all of your eggs in one basket."

"You've only given me one basket."

"Then here's another." Idiom handed him a second basket, and Quintus put eggs in both.

"How many have you taken?" Idiom asked.

"Let me see." Quintus began to count.

"Wait. Never count your chickens before they've hatched."

The Lord Treasurer rolled his eyes and they left the coop as lightning flashed above. The trio walked towards the bridge and crossed over the river. Before them towered that blue-and-white teacup. "Astonishing," Quintus remarked. "What's it for?"

The grey skies rumbled. "It's a storm in a teacup!" Ella quipped.

"Hey," Idiom said, "don't steal my thunder."

As rain pattered down, they returned to the multi-coloured mansion. "Back to the drawing board," Idiom observed as they passed the expensive painting. They went into a cramped dining room, where the table had already been laid. "Have a seat."

Ella and Quintus glanced at each other before reluctantly sitting down. Idiom pulled the cloth off to reveal a selection of bread, mustard and cakes. "Eat up."

Quintus took a slice of bread and put his knife into the mustard.

"Stop!" Idiom shouted.

Quintus paused. "Huh?"

"You don't cut the mustard."

"What? Is that meant to be an insult?"

"Oh, don't be silly," Ella interjected.

But the bearded officer seemed affronted. "Not 'cutting the mustard' is a metaphor which people use to say that someone isn't good enough."

"Put a cork in it!" Idiom snapped.

"I beg your pardon?" Quintus placed his palms on the table and glowered at the rude man.

"The mustard jar. Put the cork back in it when you're done."

Quintus muttered and did so.

"See? Piece of cake."

The Lord Treasurer sighed.

"Well? Would you like a piece of cake?" Idiom offered a slice of green sponge.

"No! I've had enough of this! You're ridiculous!" Quintus stood up and banged his head against a nail on the wall.

"You've hit the nail on the head there."

"Will you shut up?! You leave nails hanging from walls just so that you can annoy guests with your allegorical garbage? You call yourself Idiom, but I call you *Idiot!*" Quintus took off his red hat and threw it to the floor.

"You're going to leave me at the drop of a hat?"

CHAPTER 11 – THE ROCK DOVE

The sun lowered as the three regal coaches descended a winding, wooded road. The noises made by the horses and wheels disturbed the still peace of this natural world which typically hosted only the cawing of birds and flapping of their wings.

In the large middle coach, Queen Ella was accompanied by her Lord Treasurer, Quintus Northwood. Although she found the bearded man occasionally irritating, she would admit that he was a useful officer to have around. On a bench opposite them, the Bard Laureate Gullivander's quartet played some mellow evening music. In each of the four corners of the carriage sat a Veraskan guard. More of these shining female warriors protected the perimeters of the procession on horseback.

The Queen rested her head against a red-cushioned headboard inside her plush booth. Quintus munched on a plum as he glanced towards the monarch. "What has your majesty made of the national tour so far?"

"Quintus, it's not the time of day to be asking me such annoying questions. I was drifting off into a nice sleep there."

"I do apologise. I didn't realise that you would need to sleep until we reach Teffyr."

Ella rolled her eyes. "I am beginning to regret the decision to let you into my carriage. When I said that I wanted some stimulating conversation, this isn't what I had in mind." She sighed. "But anyway, why do you ask? What have you made of the national tour so far?"

Quintus plucked a stone from his mouth as he considered his own question. "I don't know. I suppose I was going to say that, well, there are a lot of odd people in our realm, aren't there? First there was that strange performer in Doff, then that purple-haired merchant, but Idiom topped the lot. Does the number of weirdoes not give rise to concern?"

The Queen's expression made her irritation obvious. "They are not weird, Quintus, nor are they strange or odd. They are interesting. My realm is perhaps the most interesting realm in the whole world."

"Right." Quintus nodded and stared thoughtfully at the floor. "I see what you mean. I may have misinterpreted the situation, though I can't get my head around why an engineer as brilliant as

Astronaemius would employ an assistant as idiotic as Idiom."

Ella shrugged. "Opposites attract, Quintus. Perhaps he needs some comedy to counteract the mathematical monotony of his work."

"I hadn't thought of that. Your majesty's wisdom never fails to astound."

Queen Ella smiled and turned her attention to Gullivander's quartet. As she jigged her head to their music, the bard suddenly played the wrong note. In fact, it was a discordance of such scale that everyone shuddered in shock. It sounded like Gully had snapped a string on his lute.

A Veraskan shouted, "Get down!" The four guardswomen stood up at the sides of the carriage; clearly, the order was to be obeyed by everyone else. An arrow struck Quintus's hat, causing the satin garb to fly off his head, and more arrows pinged against the round shields of the female defenders.

Ella shrieked and went low in her private booth where she was hidden from view. Quintus, Gullivander and his performers also got down on the floor. That discordant sound had not been the result of the bard playing a bad note. His lute had been struck by an arrow which otherwise would have pierced his arm.

Mounted Veraskans outside galloped into the woodlands to hunt the concealed attackers, while the four guardswomen inside remained for protection. The coaches moved along more speedily as the drivers sought to escape the unknown threat.

"Are they mad?!" Gullivander said, hugging the wooden floorboards of the bumping vehicle. "Who the heck would attack Veraskans?"

"The Veraskans clearly weren't their target," Quintus murmured as he clung to the decking. "And I'd be surprised if they hang around to fight. This has the hallmarks of a hit-and-run."

"Well they hit my antique lute!" the Bard Laureate bemoaned. The instrument slid along the floor as a loose string trailed behind.

"Your lute wasn't their target either," Quintus stated.

"So they were aiming for me?" Gullivander mooted.

"It's doubtful. This was most likely an assassination attempt on our fair monarch."

Ella clung to her knees, quivering in the mahogany cubicle, while some yelling could be heard in the distance. The wicked assailants were now far away and being pursued by elite horsewomen.

Gradually, those inside the carriage sat up as they sensed that the threat had passed.

Melissa, the blonde Veraskan, opened the purple curtain at the front of Ella's box and looked down at the trembling monarch. "Are you alright?"

The Queen meekly nodded. "I-I think so."

"Stand up please, so I can make sure that you haven't been hit." Ella's legs wobbled as she got up and twirled around while Melissa ran her hands along her blue dress. "You're fine."

"Where are they now?" Ella asked.

The Veraskan shrugged. "Emerald led the chase. Our drivers accelerated so we are now a safe distance away."

"Do you know who they were?" The Queen peeked through a square window, gazing at the dark woods.

"I don't, but hopefully Emerald will find out. It could have been bandits. It could have been lunatics, juvenile ruffians... I reckon there were at least six of them, based on the amount of arrows we deflected."

"Thank you," Ella said. "I will reward your courage."

"It's what we're trained for." The fair-haired guardswoman returned to the edge of the carriage and continued looking out for danger.

"We can't be too far from Teffyr now," Quintus said.

"Shall we continue with our music?" Gullivander asked as he pulled a new stringed instrument from his bag.

"Please don't," Melissa said. "I would prefer silence. We must remain vigilant."

The bard nodded and put the dulcimer away. He picked up his broken lute and plucked the arrow from it. "Would this help you discern who attacked us?"

Melissa turned and took the arrow. She held it under the glow of Melody's torchlight. "Hmm..." She shook her head. "It's a standard design."

Quintus commented, "It would be rather stupid to use trademark arrows in an anonymous assassination attempt. Bandits are the most likely culprit. They simply never go away. No matter how many strongholds we raid, how many of the brigands we imprison... They represent a continual scourge."

Melissa looked at the Lord Treasurer. "I agree, and I'm not sure if the bandits in this realm are even Celtian."

"What makes you say that?" Ella asked.

"Most of their accents are like nothing I've heard," said the Veraskan. "And, on occasions we've taken them to local settlements, for interrogation purposes, the villagers and townsfolk can rarely identify them. The bandits often claim they live in the woods but there are too many of them around. The scale of their operations seems to suggest something more co-ordinated."

Gullivander raised a finger. "May I have an input? In old tales and tomes, I have heard and seen mention of an isle of bandits. I assumed it to be fictional, because it seems so improbable and idealised. Romantic, even."

Melissa, Quintus and Ella appeared intrigued, and Gullivander posed the question, "You have not heard of the Dross Citadel?"

The others shook their heads. "I'm not saying that it exists, but it is a potential explanation for the ever-present problem of banditry. This island is said to lie somewhere in the Barbarian Sea, a cold and harsh place, forever raining. The story is that, long ago, escaped slaves from the Praetorian Empire settled there. Subsisting on seafood, they built a fort, one made out of dross. It attracted cut-throats, vagrants and outlaws from various nations. In time, it became a citadel... The Dross Citadel."

Melissa laughed. "It's far-fetched, but I'll say one thing. Most bandits round here do smell of fish."

Quintus stroked his beard. "Ones I've come across have utilised coastal caves. It would make sense if they arrived by sea."

Suddenly the carriages halted and the four guardswomen poked their heads out to see why.

A mounted Veraskan called from further up the road, "A tower." She waved her flaming torch around to illuminate the tall structure. "We should investigate."

Melissa concurred. "It's worth a look, if only to question the inhabitants. I was going to suggest a halt soon anyway, so that Emerald and the others can catch up." Melissa and Melody jumped out of the carriage.

"I want to have a look," Queen Ella said.

"Me too," Gullivander chipped in.

Melissa turned her head. "No. You stay here. Johanna and Cherry will protect you."

The short, pony-tailed figure of Melody looked at her tall comrade. "Is it any safer out here? Perhaps we shouldn't spread ourselves too thinly with our forces already split."

"Fine. If her majesty wishes to investigate this tower with us, then come along."

Ella and Gullivander stepped onto the dark road. Six armoured Veraskans surrounded them as they walked along the edge of the forest. They gazed up at the decrepit, ivy-covered tower.

The shapely metallic suits of Melissa and Melody glinted in the moonlight as they approached the obelisk-like structure, and they hacked away some thick vines hanging before the entrance. Heidi, a pigtailed Veraskan, knocked on the worn copper door. "Anyone home?"

After getting no reply, she pulled on the ring-shaped handle and the door simply jangled. "Locked, unsurprisingly."

"Give us some room," Melissa said to those standing behind the three leading ladies. Ella, Gullivander and the other Veraskans backed away. Heidi, Melody and Melissa started to shunt the rusty rectangle with their heavy bronze shields. They took turns to run at the derelict door, which rattled with every hit. After several attempts, it fell with a mighty clatter.

"Don't enter until we've given the all-clear," Heidi said. She held her axe and shield readily as she went in, flanked by two comrades.

After waiting outside for a couple of minutes, Ella looked at Gullivander. The Queen walked towards the doorway and the bard followed.

"Wait!" a Veraskan called from behind, but the pair entered. Ella's high heels tapped the leaf-covered floor of the chamber which was illuminated by Melody's torchlight. The ceiling appeared a very long way up. In fact, the tower seemed to consist of only one level, as there were no staircases.

"No human dwells here," Melissa discerned.

But a faint scuttering was heard, and Melody waved her flaming stick around as shadows moved high up.

Suddenly, a terrible screech resounded through the chamber. Ella was so startled that she did not even scream. The Veraskans turned their heads to locate the source of the sound.

Gullivander pulled his panpipes from his lips. "Sorry…"

Just as the women were about to scold the bard for his foolish behaviour, a fluttering gust flowed from above. A flock of pigeons descended and frantically made for the doorway. They flapped their wings and flew away.

Ella screamed, shielding herself with her arms. "One of them touched my hair!" The Queen seemed to be on the verge of crying. "Gullivander, you canker-headed knave! Why did you have to blow your stupid instrument?!"

"I wanted to test the acoustics." The blonde bard shrugged. "They're only pigeons, your majesty."

"Only pigeons? A pigeon is hardly different to a flying rat! Now I am probably diseased!"

"I think you owe your queen an apology," Melody told Gullivander.

"Sorry," he murmured. Ella muttered as she brushed her hair with a hand.

"Take a look at this," Heidi said. With her boot, she nudged away some dead leaves to reveal a wooden floor door. Upon finding it to be locked, she hacked it open with her axe and splinters fell onto steps beneath.

Three Veraskans descended the stairwell, followed by Queen Ella, Gullivander and three more female guards. The group found themselves in a stone chamber, one corner of which was square and the rest of which was semi-circular. On top of a pentagonal table rested a dark book, which Heidi picked up as Melody held her torch nearby.

"*The World Rose*" was the title on the front cover. Heidi opened it but found that most of the pages were irreversibly stuck together, crinkled and damp as a result of having been exposed to water for a period of time.

Queen Ella was intrigued by the title and she stepped closer while Heidi tried to flick through the manuscript. On pages which could be opened cleanly, the ink was too blurred for the words to be read. Heidi put the tome down. "Well, this tower is useless," she declared. "Let's go."

A breeze blew through the chamber and one of the tattered pages turned. Ella stared at the book and saw the murky picture of a red rose. Around its green stem was what looked like a gold snake. The text next to the picture was large and the words could be discerned despite their ink stains.

"The Sacred Rose and the World Serpent." Ella's eyes widened as she read it.

Footsteps were heard in the chamber above, so Heidi and Melissa dashed upstairs. "Emerald!"

Ella realised that the rest of the weathered hardback was ruined, so she closed it, and the group ascended the steps to the main room.

"We couldn't catch them," Emerald said, referring to the archers who her group had pursued. "Our horses had difficulty in the woods and the assailants got away. We searched for clues but found nothing."

"They didn't leave anything at the scene of the attack?" Heidi asked.

Emerald shook her head. "Nothing, besides rose petals."

"Strange. Seems that they planned things properly. You would normally expect something to be dropped on the run. Anyway, let's get out of this rotten place."

They exited the mysterious building, and Ella and Gullivander joined Quintus in the main carriage. The Veraskan guards got into position and the procession recommenced its journey to Teffyr.

"What do you know of the Order of the Sacred Rose?" Queen Ella asked Melissa.

"The what?"

Ella furrowed her brow and looked at Gullivander. "You know about them, don't you Gully?"

"Only what Ronwind told us."

Ella glanced at Quintus but he also shook his head. The Queen sighed. "Never mind." She signalled for her Bard Laureate to play some music. Gullivander's fingers danced on a fiddle as the regal carriages rumbled along the road.

After the bard finished a piece, Ella asked, "Gully, when will you perform the rest of your play *The Lily of the Valley?*" The Queen was keen to see the complete version of the floral epic which had been ruined by Duncan's antics at the World Fayre.

"I've got people working on recreating the stage props, but I have a surprise for your loveliness tomorrow at the theatre in Teffyr."

Ella's big blue eyes widened. "What is it?"

"It would defeat the purpose of being a surprise if I told you."

"You've already ruined the surprise element by telling me that there shall be a surprise."

Gully laughed. "It's another play."

"What's it called?"

The bard sighed. "*The Rock Dove.*"

It was not long before the carriages arrived at the outskirts of Teffyr. Ella peered into the glowing windows of homely thatched cottages in the sleepy town. There were not many out on the streets, as it was near midnight and the people had been told that the Queen would arrive tomorrow.

An upmarket inn had been reserved for the royal entourage. The carriages went through an iron gate and parked in the front garden of *The Blue Vine*. Staff bowed and kneeled as they greeted their esteemed guests, and Queen Ella walked over a long purple carpet to enter the gothic mansion.

Quintus suggested a quick drink before heading to bed, and Ella agreed, so they stepped onto the flowery orange fabric of a stately lounge. Gullivander's minstrels played exquisite music for their last performance of the day. Ella requested a pear juice with rum and Quintus ordered a cherry beer.

"How is it?" asked the Queen as the Lord Treasurer sipped on his red beverage.

"A little mulchy."

The next day, Queen Ella spent the morning enamouring the folk of Teffyr with her presence. In the afternoon, she went to the theatre to watch Gullivander's 'surprise' play, *The Rock Dove.*

As the monarch walked down an aisle of the square playhouse, she spotted a familiar face. It was difficult not to notice Viscount Elgar, as very few people sported such an impressive moustache. "Your highness!" exclaimed the old gent.

"Hello Sir Elgar. What a pleasant coincidence. I trust you are well."

"Indeed. I came here to buy antiques, but when I heard about this performance, couldn't miss it! Hopefully King Duncan won't steal the show this time."

Ella smiled. "He isn't actually with me, so there shouldn't be any calamities."

The audience hushed as the stage curtains opened, and the Queen sat down in the row before Viscount Elgar. The scenery depicted a simple field and a man dressed as a pigeon plodded around before turning to the audience and bewailing.

"Listen to my plight,

For I am shown disdain,
Treated like the blight,
A city-dwelling bane,
Pigeons can be seedy,
Some deserve your blame,
Most are downright greedy,
But not all are the same,
I may be less than white,
Yet I feel no shame,
For I fly in the bright light,
The Rock Dove is my name."

Cackles of laughter came from behind a holly bush. A gang of dark birds appeared and circled around the pigeon in an intimidating manner. Their ringleader wore black apparel and looked like a crow.

"This pigeon's mad,
Thinks he is a dove,
How tragically sad,
Lads, give the tramp a shove!"

A grey-hooded jackdaw stepped from the rear of the group and started to push the pigeon around. The rest of the corvine gang guffawed raucously and Jack Daw berated his victim.

"Pigeons are the worst birds,
You're all grubby scum,
So stop your silly words,
Go back to your slum!"

But the rock dove proudly stood his ground and sought to educate his bullies.

"Every pigeon is a dove,
From centuries before,
We lived in cliffs above,
So please learn your lore,
Hence my suit is grey,
Rocks are my true home,
Mountains are my way,
In the hills I roam."

Suddenly a red-haired fellow burst onto the stage. The mundane man looked out of place among the birds and the actors turned their heads in apparently real surprise. It soon became obvious that this act had not been scripted and Gullivander got up from his director's seat.

The intruder spoke, "Is her majesty here? I have a most urgent message!"

Ella stood up, holding the lower ends of her mauve gown, and when the ginger man sighted the monarch, he rushed towards her.

"Your majesty's realm is on the brink of invasion!"

CHAPTER 12 – COLUMNS IN THE CAULIFLOWER

People in the theatre audience gasped as they heard the serious words of the man interrupting the play. Queen Ella studied his brown garb and noticed that he wore the badge of the Royal Scouts which meant that he was genuine.

The messenger continued, "A large fleet in the Azure heads for our coastline at the latitude of Livia. Merchant vessels and fishermen sighted at least twenty ships, many carrying soldiers. By now, they have probably reached our shores."

Ella gaped silently for a few moments. "What insignia do they bear?"

"It is unknown, but their colours are blue and yellow."

Ella suddenly thought of the bright blue-and-yellow procession which had entered her tent at the World Fayre. The Queen turned to her Veraskan guards who had been listening attentively.

"Emerald, with your fastest horsewomen, find Nina Veraska and tell her to bring her entire army to Livia's main barracks. We are under attack by the Assyrian Empire."

Emerald, knowledgeable about the world's empires, tilted her head. "The Assyrians? Here? That makes no sense."

"It does make sense because they have threatened me before!" Ella retorted, not wishing to explain the situation regarding her crown jewels. "But never you mind about politics."

"Very well." The flame-haired guardswoman turned and left the theatre with some comrades.

"Melissa, go with utmost haste to the capital and give Dungeon Hark the same instructions."

The blonde lass nodded and departed. The Queen and the remaining Veraskans hurried to their carriages and set off for Celtia's primary city.

As monarch, Ella was technically the commander-in-chief of her armed forces, but she had little understanding of military matters. The realm had not been involved in a war for three decades and the Queen barely knew the capabilities of her armies.

The journey from Teffyr to Livia took three hours, but it was unlikely that the invaders had reached the capital yet because it was twenty miles inland. Queen Ella arrived at the extensive barracks complex on the southern edge of the city. A raven-haired figure sat on a black horse in front of a great square of green-and-purple soldiers. Dungeon Hark had mobilised his men swiftly, but the Veraskan forces would take longer because they were stationed in woodlands ten miles to the west.

"As you are probably aware by now, our realm is being invaded by the Assyrian Empire," Ella told Dungeon.

The middle-aged man nodded. "Indeed, I have heard."

"How many regular foot soldiers do you have?"

"Two thousand, your majesty."

The Queen regarded the formation of troops, who wore chainmail, round helmets, oval shields and long swords. "And cavalry?"

"Four hundred, your majesty." The horse soldiers could be seen preparing in a nearby field. Optimised for speed and offense, they wore leather and carried sabres which were thinner than the infantry's swords.

The Master of the Armoury, Sir Terin Cormin, provided Queen Ella with a silvery suit of armour, a bejewelled sword and a light grey horse. In her youth, Ella had been a keen equestrian, but she had not ridden for years. She was less comfortable carrying a weapon but hoped that she would not have to use it.

A young scout appeared and addressed Queen Ella and Dungeon Hark. "The enemy is within five miles of the east gate of Livia. They move in four great columns, each containing about three thousand men."

Ella swayed, seeming to nearly faint. She looked at Dungeon, as though he would know what to do. "They have twelve thousand men?" Dungeon asked, to confirm what he thought he had just heard.

"Yes, my Lord."

"We have but a quarter of their numbers," the commander stated.

The Queen inquired of the scout, "Do they have cavalry?"

The brown-haired boy shook his head. "No, your majesty. Their ships seem to have brought only men, not horses."

Ella turned to Dungeon. "Do you know how many the Veraskans have?"

"Only about seven hundred infantry and two hundred cavalry."

"Well, we know that each Veraskan is worth five normal troops," Queen Ella said.

Dungeon furrowed his brow. "Veraskans are indeed fine soldiers, your majesty, but I am not sure if they are worth five. Even if they were, we would still be heavily outnumbered. We also know nothing of the quality of our opponent. Our cavalry might be a secret weapon but they will eventually be overwhelmed."

The Queen raised her amethyst staff. "You shall deploy your men immediately in the farmland east of the city and hold off the enemy until the Veraskans arrive."

Dungeon seemed hesitant. "Your majesty, should we not wait for the Veraskans to arrive before we enter into battle? Surely our only chance of victory is if we stand together as one force. Would it not be wiser to go within the city walls? We could wait there for the Veraskans while our archers attack the enemy from the ramparts."

"How will we meet the Veraskans if we are hiding in Livia?" Ella said. "By that time, the Assyrians would have surrounded our capital, and our archers would be too thinly spread to deal with an army of twelve thousand. The enemy would find a way in, or they would simply besiege the city and starve us to death. If we sit and do nothing, then not only do we show weakness, but we are really waiting for our demise. Is attack not the best form of defence? That is what my father used to say."

Dungeon nodded. "I receive your majesty's wisdom, but then, instead of hiding in Livia, would it not be better to wait in the western woods? That way, we could gather information about our enemy, perhaps even let them take the city, and strike once the Veraskans are with us?"

"This city will not be used as bait." The Queen looked at the walls of Livia. "I shall not sacrifice my citizens. If we let the heart of my realm be captured, then we have already been defeated. You will prevent our capital from falling into the enemy's hands at all costs, and your best chance of doing so is with troops on the field. The city's archers will aid you from the east wall. You only need to withstand the Assyrians until the Veraskans arrive, which will not be long because they are marching here with great haste. The longer you hesitate, Dungeon, the graver our situation becomes."

She continued, "Remember your oath, which you and your soldiers took, in which you swore that you would die for this realm if required to. The alternative is to become a foreign dominion of an empire far crueller than my own. Your army exists to defend my nation, and defend it you shall. If you succeed in this task, you will be honoured in Celtia for the rest of your days, but if you fail, you will still be remembered as the heroes who tried to save us."

Dungeon appeared moved by his monarch's rousing speech as he finally came round. The raven-haired commander turned to face his men. "To the east fields!"

The soldiers marched dutifully to the vast cauliflower field which sloped down from Livia's east wall. Dungeon ordered his infantry to form one long column, four hundred troops across and five ranks deep. Such a sight would give any approaching army food for thought, and Dungeon hoped that when the Assyrians saw the great green-and-purple line from the distance, they would hesitate enough to give the Veraskans time to arrive.

Dungeon ordered his cavalry to split into two groups and go into the forests which verged on both sides of the cauliflower field. "As soon as you hear my bugle, attack their flanks." Two hundred horses cantered down to the woods on the column's right and the same number went to the left.

It was a fine day. An occasional breeze coursed through the farmlands, making the green-and-purple banner in the middle of the regiment flutter. Only the cawing of crows broke the eerie silence which fell upon the soldiers as they waited for their enemy.

Then they came as a wave of blue and yellow cresting a distant hill. Thirty lines of one hundred each descended through pastureland two miles before the defenders. It was as impressive a sight as Dungeon's entire army, and that was just the first column. After a gap, the second column appeared, looking identical to the first.

In the midst of the third column sat King Sennacherib upon his elevated throne. Only the monarch seemed to have any identity in this horde, not because he had much personality, but because all of his subjects appeared exactly the same, like insentient shoals of fish.

Every one of them wore a peaked jonquil helmet, just like those guards who had come to the World Fayre. Ella imagined that they also wore the eye shadow and earrings which she saw that day, and she asked herself how such silly-looking men could be effective soldiers.

The Queen took up a position on the city wall, which was lined with archers and catapults. From there, she would have a good view of the battlefield and still be able to communicate with Dungeon below.

A mounted messenger galloped along the outside of the wall and stopped when he saw Queen Ella above. "Your highness, I have news that Viscount Elgar of Cosgrove is on his way with cavalry. He wishes to aid in the defence of your realm and should be here within the hour."

The Queen's eyebrows rose in surprise. Dungeon too appeared lifted by the news. "That old gentleman is full of surprises," Ella said. "See, there is reason to hope. If we can stave off the enemy for an hour, then the Veraskans and Elgar's cavalry will be with us. And who knows what other forces might come to our assistance."

Dungeon nodded, though he did not quite share the same level of optimism. Ella continued, "We shall fight through the day and night, for weeks if necessary. And if our military succumbs, I know that the citizens of Celtia will take up arms themselves. The farmers, blacksmiths, merchants, bards and yeomen; they too will defend this realm when they see it under attack."

Dungeon nodded again. Such boundless idealism was inspiring. There was certainly no use in being pessimistic at this stage. The four enemy columns continued to advance and their front reached the bottom of the cauliflower field. The Assyrians made their lines longer by spreading out, thinning in depth, so that they could cope with Dungeon's lengthy formation.

The raven-haired commander lifted an arm and four catapults hurled boulders at the invaders. They made ripples in the sea of blue and yellow. An enemy horn blared and the first column charged up the cauliflower field.

Dungeon's men held their shields in defensive mode as the thunder of Assyrian sandals grew louder, while the city archers hailed the enemy with arrows.

The rear of the first Assyrian column stopped and it became apparent that these were archers. They aimed their bows and fired at the city parapets. Queen Ella ducked and went into a tower above the gatehouse, from where she could watch the battle through a narrow slit.

Dungeon shouted and his men stormed down the slope. The din of war began as green-and-purple met blue-and-yellow. They were about the same length and width, but the Assyrians would surely soon bring in their second column to make their numerical advantage count. Arrows flew over the heads of the infantry as the two sets of archers engaged in their own ranged skirmish.

Meanwhile, four hundred horsemen hid in the woods on either side of the field. Dungeon was disciplined enough to wait for the perfect tactical moment, which was about to come. As the second Assyrian column charged, Dungeon blew his bugle and his cavalry appeared. Galloping hooves rumbled through the farmlands as two squadrons rushed for the flanks and rear of the enemy.

Panic broke out in the Assyrian ranks and they lost their disciplined shape. The Celtian cavalry decimated their perimeters as the second column became a rabble.

Beyond the bottom of the cauliflower field, the third and fourth Assyrian columns halted. It appeared that King Sennacherib was uncertain of how to proceed. Dungeon had executed his strategies perfectly. Perhaps the enemy was no longer prepared to throw men into the fray. If the regular cavalry could wreak such havoc, the Veraskan horsewomen could surely do more.

But it became apparent that King Sennacherib was not dithering after all. He was simply reshuffling his army. From the rear to the front of the third column, a thick line of archers stepped forward. A horn sounded and the ragtag of the second column ducked low simultaneously. The cavalry in their midst were suddenly exposed and a volley of arrows flew at them.

Horses started to fall upon the bodies of Assyrians. Some tried to flee sideways, which only made them larger targets. Within minutes, Dungeon's cavalry was cut to pieces. A small number managed to escape to the woods from where they had boldly charged not long before.

The cauliflower field had swiftly been cleared of horses. What little remained of the second Assyrian column rallied and surged forward to bolster their front ranks. Suddenly things looked very dark for the courageous defenders.

CHAPTER 13 – ARMY OF TWEED

The Queen's mood had swung dramatically, but as she stared down at the battlefield, she received some great news. The Veraskans had arrived and they were at Livia's southeast tower.

Ella descended into the interior of the wall, rushed through stone corridors and went up to a balcony, from where she saw a group of armoured women on the ground.

"Nina! How wonderful it is to see you. Your women can now save Dungeon's wavering men!"

The Veraskan leader looked up at the Queen. "We cannot enter such a battle and emerge victorious."

Ella appeared baffled. "What?"

"Surely you can see it yourself. In their rear columns alone, the Assyrians have six thousand troops. I have seven hundred infantry and two hundred cavalry."

"What are you talking about? You're Veraskans!"

"Veraskans are not invincible," said Nina.

"Then go and charge the flanks and rear of those already engaged," demanded the Queen. "Your soldiers will cut them down quickly, and the enemy king will see that we have hidden reserves of elite units. He will withdraw his last two columns and retreat."

Nina shook her head. "He will simply throw those columns at us, and overwhelm us, and there will be nothing left of your army or your realm by the end of it."

Queen Ella looked appalled by such icy pessimism. "What sort of a Veraskan are you! Go and join that battle right now!"

Just as Nina was about to reply, a thunder of hooves came from the trail to the south. A band of horsemen appeared, led by the unmistakable, moustached figure of Viscount Elgar. He wore a moss green checked tweed suit and a brown leather deerstalker hat. A smell of whisky wafted from the mounted regiment.

"Sir Elgar!" Ella waved her arms.

He bowed from the top of his mottled grey stallion. "I have come to assist the defence of your realm!"

"Your timing is impeccable! Our men on the field face defeat, but with your cavalry and these great Veraskans, they can be saved!"

"It shall be done!" said the old man.

Nina Veraska questioned, "How many horses do you have?"

"Eighty!"

"*Eighty?* That's nothing. And your men don't appear to be armoured… Your swords look like they were built for fencing."

Ella's grin turned into a frown as she looked over Elgar's horsemen, most of whom were dressed in tweed and other couth garments. They looked ready for a hunt rather than a battle.

"We are a swift offensive unit!" Elgar declared exuberantly. He waved his slender sabre around, slashing and thrusting as the curled ends of his hoary moustache bounced. "We shall cut the enemy to pieces before they even realise that we are unarmoured!"

Nina noticed that some of the horsemen were holding musical instruments. "You seem to have as many musicians as fighters."

"Nonsense! They're all fighters. They will take up their weapons at the appropriate time. Music is important in battle. It will inspire us." The gentleman raised his sword and his ensemble began to play a bold and uplifting string piece.

"I have won many battles, but never to music," Nina said. "It can be a distraction from the reality of the situation."

"Let me show myself by my actions, not my words!" The viscount looked up at the Queen. "What is the situation, your highness?"

Ella gazed towards the cauliflower field. "The last lines of our infantry are valiantly repelling the enemy, but they will soon be overwhelmed. Behind them, the Assyrians have two large columns of reinforcements."

"I've got a plan that will knock 'em," Elgar said, "knock 'em flat." He turned to Nina. "You shall relieve those fighting men and I shall deal with the rear columns."

"Those rear columns are six thousand strong," Nina said. "You will defeat them with your mounted orchestra?"

The viscount ignored her and turned to his cavalry. "Now then gentleman, *you play this tune as though you've never heard it before!*"

Suddenly they erupted into a marvellously momentous military march. Elgar pulled on the reins of his steed and galloped down a wooded track. His eighty horsemen followed as they performed their ebullient music.

Nina appeared almost offended by the old man's reckless audacity. "He won't even have the element of surprise, as the enemy will hear them. Every one of them will die. What a waste of life."

The Queen frowned as she peered towards the farmlands. The third enemy column was moving slowly forward, to join the battle and deliver the final blow to Dungeon's army. Ella and Nina could both see the distant fourth column, which contained the rotund figure of King Sennacherib. They watched and waited in grim fascination for Elgar's band to appear.

"Why don't you do something?" Queen Ella snapped at Nina. "You complain about them wasting their lives, but it is only a waste if you stand here and do nothing. Do not let it be a waste. Let it be a useful distraction while you attack!"

"This distraction will not last more than a minute. I can achieve nothing in that time."

Elgar's cavalry emerged from woods and charged straight at the left flank of the Assyrian fourth column. Within seconds, the tide of moss green was upon the blue-and-yellow rectangle, which wobbled. The viscount's horsemen surged down both the front and back of the enemy formation, engulfing it like a wave. Peaked jonquil hats flew through the air amidst a whirlwind of slashing sabres as Elgar swished his sword around like the conductor of an orchestra performing the dramatic rondo of a symphony.

The small army of tweed penetrated the bewildered mass of footmen. Such cold-blooded courage, astonishing quickness and attacking finesse had created a mass hysteria in the Assyrian ranks. Ella and Nina watched as soldiers scattered and the regiment lost all form.

"Incredible," said Nina. "They have created an impression of greater numbers than they have. Their power is entirely illusory, but they have broken the enemy, who probably expect another wave of cavalry to emerge at any moment. Because no army of eighty horsemen would attack three thousand soldiers, but now they attack a mob of individuals rather than a unit, so they have the advantage." The cynical Veraskan leader spoke about warfare as though it was a science.

Queen Ella gaped. "Are you going to do something now then?"

Nina looked at her women and then called a war cry. The armoured flock began to run towards the battlefield.

Dungeon was down to his last line of infantry. About four hundred troops were locked in combat with three times their number. The raven-haired commander would soon be forced to throw himself into the fray, and he would die a hero.

But just as the swarm of blue-and-yellow started to envelop the green-and-purple, a cavalry squadron appeared. Bronze-and-gold horsewomen swooped like eagles along the backs of the Assyrians as Veraskan axe-heads rained down.

Dungeon's men were invigorated by the sight of those shining female warriors and suddenly they too fought like gladiators. Some startled Assyrian soldiers were so stunned by the resurgence of their opponents that they surrendered on the spot. The remnants of the first and second columns finally crumbled.

But the glistening, untouched third column shuffled beyond. Just as they had previously done to deal with cavalry, the Assyrians brought their line of archers to the fore. Veraskans knew only one way of dealing with such a quandary. They turned to face their foe. As the first wave of arrows flew at them, the mounted warriors charged. Some fell, but the thundering onslaught swiftly assailed the archers and destroyed them in moments.

Behind, ranks of Assyrian soldiers stormed forward. Two-and-a-half thousand men could take on two hundred women on horses, they thought. But from the trees roared a cacophony of female cries as the Veraskan infantry appeared. Seven hundred elite women attacked the side of the regiment and rapidly wrapped round its rear. It was a practised Veraskan manoeuvre which they delivered with devastating efficiency.

These glittering warriors displayed all the prowess, dexterity and courage for which they were famed, fighting like the mythical guardians of a celestial sanctuary. The Assyrian third column split, as half continued to rush ahead while half halted to fight the tide of bronze-and-gold infantry.

The Veraskans chipped away at the edges of the broken block as calmly and expertly as a sculptor would work on a piece of stone. After several minutes of picking and probing, the slab began to give way, and then it shattered. Once again, the Assyrians lost all shape as they were defeated by a force numerically inferior but otherwise superior. Instead of running away, these soldiers dropped their weapons and raised their hands. Perhaps they thought that female warriors were more likely to be forgiving than male ones.

Dungeon's men brought ropes and chains to bind the surrendering enemy. The prisoners of war were marched into the city while medics

and nurses came out of Livia's gates. They treated as many of their
wounded as they could, carrying some away on stretchers.

Just over three hundred of Dungeon's exhausted troops remained.
They had fought longer and harder than anyone else, so their
commander allowed them to rest. The Veraskans had four hundred
infantry and one hundred cavalry left. Their actions may have
appeared effortless but they too had suffered significant casualties.

Suddenly Viscount Elgar came cantering up the field with seven of
his cavalry. His tweed jacket was torn and blood-stained, his hair
hatless and messy. The old man panted, requiring a few moments to
compose himself before he could speak.

"Thought we had those ruffians. Vanquished a thousand, but they
rallied."

The group gazed across the farmlands and saw the ravaged
remains of the fourth column moving down a distant hill as grey
clouds hung above. Nina looked at Viscount Elgar, amazed that his
eighty horsemen had sown such devastation. "Well done. We can
finish them off." The Veraskan chief was confident that her troops
could handle the last jaded enemy soldiers. Elgar grinned and tried to
flatten his ruffled hair with a hand.

"Where is their king?" asked Queen Ella. "I cannot see him in that
column."

Elgar shrugged. "I suppose they must've managed to get him away.
We were tied up with the main pack."

The fat Sennacherib would be helpless without his army anyway.
The heroic defenders watched as the tattered remnant of the Assyrian
regiment marched for a while but then stopped.

"Seems they aren't going to take us on after all," said Nina
Veraska. "Come on!" she taunted, even though the enemy was too
far away to hear.

Suddenly, over the hill emerged another column. Nina's brash
taunts ceased and she turned her wrath on Elgar. "You fool! You
didn't vanquish any of them! That looks like an entire regiment!"

Elgar appeared bewildered. "We vanquished at least one thousand,
as a conservative estimate."

Dungeon Hark spoke up, "That is a new column. You can tell
because they are all still wearing their hats."

Ella, Nina, Dungeon and Elgar stared at the glistening army on the
hilltop. It felt like time had been turned back to that portentous

moment when the enemy first appeared.

Nina scowled at Queen Ella. "You said there were only four columns!"

"There were," Ella replied from the ramparts. "However, a smaller group of ships was sighted behind the main fleet. I suppose they must have brought more troops."

"Why didn't you tell us this?!"

"I didn't want to scare you. You almost abandoned me earlier."

This new fifth column caught up with the remainder of the fourth, merging to become one column of approximately four thousand. Then came a sixth column, in the middle of which sat King Sennacherib upon his dazzling throne.

"Their empire is infinite," said Dungeon, his voice edgy like he was on the verge of a breakdown. "How can we stand against them? The quality of their tactics and the skill of their soldiers are irrelevant if they can hurl wave after wave. We cannot win a war of attrition."

Nina threw her axe to the ground. "Surrender is our only option now. If we accept defeat and wave the white flag, they might let us live. If we continue to fight, they will show us no mercy."

Queen Ella raged. "Do you want to be a prisoner or a slave? I would rather die than be conquered!" She flailed her arms. "There will be no surrender! We shall surprise them, just as we did before, with flanking cavalry charges!"

"Soon we will have no cavalry left," Nina riposted. "At the very most, we could engage one regiment of three thousand and may somehow fluke victory. But seven thousand is impossible. And for all we know, there are another ten thousand on their way."

Dungeon and Elgar said nothing. The Assyrian front line reached the foot of the pastureland and would soon be in the cauliflower field. Then any delusions of hope vanished as a seventh column appeared some way behind the other two.

"Their king is mad," barked Nina. "How many soldiers does he think he needs to conquer this little realm?"

Dungeon turned to his monarch. "I request that my forces withdraw. They have fought valiantly and have nothing left to give. I will not send them to their slaughter. I doubt that they would even obey the order."

Ella gaped in silence, eyes welling with tears.

"Wait," Viscount Elgar said suddenly.

"Wait for what, you fool?" snapped Nina. "The only thing we wait for now is our demise."

"Wait," repeated the old man. "Those are not the Assyrian colours."

Nina looked at the faraway column. "Well no, clearly not. They are obviously their elite unit."

Ella squinted as she gazed at the distant formation of soldiers. Their silvery suits were adorned with red and in their midst was a giant crimson banner. They carried huge rectangular shields rather than the Assyrian circular ones.

"Praetorians," murmured Dungeon. The overcast skies crackled.

CHAPTER 14 – A SCARLET SUNRISE

The Queen rode out of the east gate of Livia to join the brave heroes assembled in the cauliflower field. They watched as a Praetorian legion moved down a distant hill above two Assyrian columns.

"Caesar has sent his troops," remarked Viscount Elgar, "but are they friend or foe?"

Ella declared, "Caesar said that he would do anything for me. He told me that if my realm was ever invaded, he would send his legions."

"Well," Nina Veraska commented, "it looks to me like they are allies. They must have come to an agreement to carve up this continent between themselves, starting with your realm."

"Oh, cease your pessimism!" said Elgar. "I find it most unattractive."

Nina's cheeks flared red. She was just about to respond when they saw the Praetorian legion charge. The tired defenders of Celtia watched in awe as two mighty empires clashed in the farmlands east of their capital. Even from this distance, they could hear the clashes of metal, thuds and screams.

The long rectangle of silver-and-red began to push the blue-and-yellow down the hill. The two Assyrian columns formed one vast square which was considerably thicker than the one opposing it.

"Perhaps we should help them," Viscount Elgar suggested. Lightning struck the skies, the clouds rumbled and a heavy rain started. Dungeon Hark looked at his men, who were watching the battle with keen interest, and then glanced at Nina. "I will if she does."

Nina analysed the epic encounter for a few more moments. "Well, I suppose if we help the Praetorians, they are less likely to attack us afterwards. I know how fickle men can be, especially powerful ones." The Veraskan chief picked up her axe.

Elgar chuckled. "I would suggest a cavalry charge at their rear."

"Sounds good to me." Nina finally agreed with someone. "Simple and effective. Want to lead my cavalry, old man?"

The moustached maestro looked quite astonished. "Why, certainly. Thank you." He went to the Veraskan cavalry with his seven tweedy horsemen. "Now then ladies. Let us show the enemy the meaning of offensive yet refined vulgarity!"

The mounted warriors cantered down the field and the Veraskan infantry marched behind them. Dungeon's regular soldiers followed and Queen Ella also rode out cautiously.

Once the cavalry were within striking distance, they began to gallop through the torrential downpour. Predictably, the mere sound of their approach created panic in the Assyrian rear, and that panic would ripple through their ranks. Some soldiers tried to squeeze their way forward while others sought refuge in nearby woods.

After eroding the back of the enemy block with their first charge, the cavalry regrouped and surged again. It had become a routine exercise, delivered with superb effectiveness under the genius command of Viscount Elgar. The wave of horses ebbed and cascaded in a particularly potent and penetrating charge which shattered the Assyrian formation.

Their front line was being destroyed by skilled Praetorian troops. The disciplined legion soon enveloped their opponent on three sides, and then there was nowhere for the Assyrians to run. The battle turned into a massacre.

In the midst of it all was hefty King Sennacherib upon his elevated throne. His forces were packed so tightly around him that his chair began to totter, and then it crashed to the ground. The elderly sovereign would not get up again.

By the time the Veraskan infantry arrived, it was already over. Two thousand Assyrian soldiers threw down their weapons in surrender. The Praetorians immediately started binding them.

Viscount Elgar trotted past one group of captives. "Where are you taking them?"

"To our ships," said a Praetorian captain.

"What will happen to them then?"

"They will become labourers in our empire."

Gradually the farmlands were cleared of Assyrians. Veraskans scoured the fields while Dungeon's soldiers combed the surrounding woods.

Some three thousand Praetorians stood in a wide semi-circle. Lightning flashed as Queen Ella rode up to the crescent of iron and crimson, rain-drenched hair sweeping behind her. The light grey horse halted and she raised her amethyst staff.

"I, Queen Ella Tundra of Celtia, thank you, honourable legionaries of Praetoria, for coming to our assistance today. Who is your commander, that I may speak to?"

The middle of the crescent parted and a man wearing a red-crested, gilded helmet walked forward. The rain bounced off his breastplate, upon which were the golden wings of an eagle. Behind him flowed a scarlet cape.

The legionary took off his helmet and his thick, matted hair sprung free. His amber eyes seemed to glow as he gazed at the mounted maiden.

"Caesar!" Ella got off her horse, ran towards the scarlet emperor and embraced him.

"You seem surprised. Did I not tell you that I would send my legions if ever your realm was invaded?"

"You did. I remember, but I suppose I did not expect you to actually come yourself. Oh Caesar, I cannot thank you enough! How did you know about the invasion?"

"We saw their fleet heading your way, and I knew about the situation between you and Sennacherib. It was also an opportunity for me. One of my rivals now lies dead." Caesar gestured to the upturned teal-and-gold throne of the Assyrian King. "We have burned their ships and wrecked their army. The Assyrian Empire will now crumble, and soon all of their lands will belong to me."

"Fantastic!" Ella smiled. "I can accommodate you and your legion here for as long as you require."

"Thank you. That would be most welcome, but we won't need to stay for more than one night."

The scarlet emperor signalled for his men to follow and the great legion moved towards Livia. Most of the Celtian forces were already on their way there. A loud thunder rumbled through the farmlands as a deluge of rain descended upon the bodies of the fallen.

Jubilant crowds greeted the victors as they walked through the east gate of Livia. People hugged and kissed Dungeon and his soldiers, Nina and her Veraskans, and Viscount Elgar. The noise erupted when Queen Ella rode in.

A triumphant fanfare of horns, harps and drums heralded the entry of Caesar's army into the capital. The Praetorian Emperor was now wearing his laurel crown as he strutted along imperiously. The citizens were amazed by the sight of this legendary legion on their streets, for these were the all-conquering, invincible soldiers of the world's greatest civilization. The folk of Livia gave them food, drink, gifts and gold, while accommodation was arranged in the barracks, halls and inns.

Queen Ella and Gaius Romulus Caesar ascended the steps of the Marble Palace. Marble was the favoured stone of Praetoria so the emperor felt quite at home. They went into the pillared entrance chamber and Ella took Caesar up a flight of stairs to show him his luxurious quarters.

"There is going to be a banquet in the hall for today's heroes," Ella mentioned.

Caesar turned his head. "Am I not the only hero?"

"You are certainly one hero, Caesar, and I am incredibly grateful."

They stepped into the master bedroom of the Marble Palace, a lavish white chamber with a four-poster bed in its centre and a sculpture of a dove in one corner. Caesar studied the room for a few moments. His scarlet cape flourished as he turned to face Ella. "If I had not arrived, the Assyrians would have conquered your realm."

The Queen of Celtia paused as she studied the Praetorian Emperor, her lips drawing into a line before she spoke. "That is true. But others also fought valiantly, and for many hours while staring doom in the face." She thought about the efforts of Dungeon's men, Elgar and the Veraskans.

"Then let them have their banquet downstairs, and let us have ours up here. We are sovereigns."

Ella stared at the table pensively. She certainly wanted to partake in the banquet, but she did not want to offend Caesar. He had a large legion in Livia and it seemed imprudent to disagree with the most powerful man in the world.

"Very well," Ella finally replied. "That sounds nice. I will notify our staff."

The scarlet emperor smiled. "When shall we meet?"

"In about an hour. I will come here."

"Perfect." Caesar went into the bathroom to clean himself.

Ella went downstairs and found Elgar, Dungeon and Nina enjoying champagne in the great hall. "Hello my heroes. There will be a banquet here for you soon. Unfortunately I cannot come, because I have urgent matters to attend to. There will also be a ceremony tomorrow, in which I will show my appreciation for everything that you have done."

Elgar offered Ella a glass. "At least have a drink with us."

She glanced at the sparkling white wine. "I am very sorry but there are some important things that I have to deal with. A monarch is always busy. Enjoy the feast."

Ella went up to an en-suite room and had a bath. Candles flickered around her as she relaxed in the water, after which she put on a purple dress, two amethyst earrings and tied her hair in a bun. She looked surprisingly fresh for a ruler whose realm had almost been conquered today.

Ella stepped into the corridor and saw that the door to Caesar's room was ajar, so she knocked once and entered. Gaius Romulus was clad in a white toga adorned with a scarlet stripe. He wore his leafy crown upon his hair which appeared fluffy after being washed.

"Hello." The Praetorian Emperor bounced a red apple in his hand.

"Hello Caesar." They moved to a candlelit table, upon which was a selection of dishes; a glorious seafood platter, olive bread, fish soup, a grand petal salad and many cheeses and fruits. Caesar picked up a jug and poured red wine into two silver goblets.

"Thank you." Ella quickly took a sip while Caesar reclined in his chair and had a great gulp. When the goblet left his mouth, there was a crimson hue on his lips.

"You look beautiful," Caesar stated forthrightly as he gazed across the table.

"Thank you." Ella returned his gaze.

"I did not just come here to save your realm. I also brought a gift." The emperor conjured up a sparkling pearl necklace.

Ella stared at the glinting spheres. "Oh, how beautiful!"

Caesar walked over to Ella and put the adornment around her neck. "This is not the first wonderful gift that you have given me. I would have gotten you something if I had known you were coming."

"Your company suffices," said Caesar, returning to his seat.

A thought suddenly occurred to Ella. "Did you send me that letter?"

"What letter?"

"The one with a picture of a rose on it."

"No. I did not."

"Oh, I thought it might have been you because the words seemed like the sort of thing that you would say."

Caesar seemed intrigued. "What did they say?"

"That I am the Rose of the World." Ella remembered how Caesar had once called her that at the World Fayre.

Caesar shrugged. "I would say that I am the Rose of the World." He pointed to his red colours and grinned.

Ella frowned, and Caesar realised his faux-pas. "You are more like a lavender flower," he added, gesturing to her purple colours.

Detecting a need to impress her now, the scarlet emperor glanced at a basket of fruits on the table. "I am the red apple and you are the purple plum." A slight smile played on Ella's lips. "I am the ruby and you are the amethyst." Caesar looked at a vase of flowers nearby. "I am the crimson carnation and you are the lilac lily."

Ella now seemed interested, but Caesar's poetic rhetoric was not yet finished. "I am the scarlet sunrise and you are the violet sunset. Without my sunrise, there would be no day, but without your sunset, there would be no night. Yet the sun can only rise if it has fallen, and it can only fall if it has risen. So we cannot exist without each other, for every sunrise requires its sunset."

Ella's bosom rose and fell. "But they say the sun never sets on your empire, Caesar."

"That is why I need you." Caesar's keen amber gaze locked onto Ella's deep blue oceanic hue. He stood up, reached for the vase of flowers and took out a crimson carnation and a lilac lily. He spread the petals of the carnation and placed the lily within it. "Fair Queen Lily, be my Empress of the World." Caesar handed Ella the double flower.

Her eyes widened and her dainty body swayed. "I..." Ella's lips quivered. "I... Th-That is a very kind offer, Caesar, but I would need time to think about your proposal. I could not possibly answer such an important question right now."

The scarlet emperor slowly withdrew his hand. "What is there to think about? I possess all the riches in the world. The smallest province of my empire is greater than the entirety of your realm. When you see Praetoria, you will wonder if you have not transcended the mortal plane and walk among Gods. For you will see art and architecture of a celestial culture, and you will learn the true meaning of civilization. I can show you the tallest trees, the sweetest fruits, as we walk through the gardens of paradise. I can offer you Heaven on Earth."

Ella swallowed. "I am sorry, Romulus. You are a good man, but I just can't deal with this right now." She sighed. "My realm was almost destroyed today, and I have a lot of things going on."

Caesar turned around and knocked a silver goblet off the table. It was unclear whether it was accidental or deliberate, but the item crashed against the floor and the sound caused staff to enter the chamber. Ella slipped out of the door, and went to her room, where she collapsed on the bed.

CHAPTER 15 – THE WHITE ROOM

In the morning, Ella stepped out of her bedchamber and saw Gaius Romulus Caesar in the marble corridor. He was already dressed in his full regalia, that shining armour of red, iron and gold.

"Caesar, are you coming to the victory ceremony today, so that you can receive a medal?"

"No. I must return to Praetoria. My empire cannot last for long without me."

"I understand. Well, I really cannot thank you enough for saving my realm. Hopefully I will see you again soon."

Caesar turned. The last that Ella saw of him was his scarlet cape waving behind him as he walked down the white hallway.

In the afternoon, the Queen of Celtia appeared on the great balcony of the Marble Palace. The amethyst jewel of her staff glinted in the sun and the broad street below was packed with adoring citizens. It was just like Ella's coronation, except that today she was even more popular. In the eyes of the people, she was now a brilliant military commander whose tactical genius had held off the numerically superior Assyrian regiments, while her diplomatic skills had ensured the allegiance of Praetoria. Of course, Ella knew that she had only played a tiny part in yesterday's victory, and the purpose of this ceremony was to salute those who were responsible.

First, there was a ten-minute silence to honour those brave soldiers who had made the ultimate sacrifice. In the cauliflower field to the east, the dead were still being collected. The Queen announced that a vast cemetery and permanent memorial would be constructed there.

Trumpets flared as Dungeon Hark stepped onto the balcony. The raven-haired commander thought about the speech that Queen Ella had given him yesterday. She had said that he would become a hero of the people, and today he felt like one. The purple monarch kissed the staunch defender, placing a gold medal around his neck and giving him a bouquet of flowers, which he threw to the crowds. Dungeon went down to lead a parade of his three hundred surviving soldiers along the streets. Without their unfaltering courage, the city would have capitulated early on.

Nina Veraska appeared on the balcony. Ella had found her difficult to work with yesterday, but when she did finally commit, her elite women fought superbly. Nina also received a gold medal and a bouquet and marched her troops through the city. Folk were enraptured by the sight of those powerful female warriors in their glistening bronze-and-gold armours. The Veraskans had lost half their numbers in the battle, making it the largest loss in their history.

Next onto the balcony was Viscount Elgar, that old maestro whose timely arrival, bold optimism and sheer audacity had salvaged the operation when it appeared doomed. He still wore his tattered, blood-stained tweed suit, but his hair was now immaculately combed to the side and his thick moustache looked finer than ever. The Queen gave Elgar the same awards and kissed his cheek. He put an arm around her and said, "You must come to my country house. My daughters would love to meet you."

Ella smiled. "I will." The viscount led his band of mounted gentlemen down the streets, those seven which remained of the eighty who had come with him from Cosgrove. Unfortunately, most of their musical instruments had been wrecked in the fighting, so they could not perform a triumphal tune, but Gullivander's orchestra played the national anthem. The blonde bard gave an ode to end the ceremony.

"Today they are adored,
This band of bronze and tweed,
And there is no reward,
To match their gallant deed,
They faced a heinous horde,
One motivated by greed,
But each troop held their sword,
No matter how they did bleed,
Doom they charged toward,
Fought with skill and speed,
Until freedom was restored,
With valour they did succeed."

Thousands had died, but the epic victory inspired a new wave of patriotism in the realm. A stream of eager recruits signed up to the military in the days after the great battle. Replacing the fallen Veraskans would be harder, because each of them trained from infancy and received years of specialist schooling.

Indeed, the near disaster was a sign that more attention ought be given to the hitherto neglected armed forces. The regular corps deserved improvement and expansion, for they had shown themselves to be as hardy as, and more dependable than, the Veraskans. An increase in budget allocation to military matters would be required, so Ella called a meeting with her Lord Treasurer when she returned to the Tundra Castle.

Clad in a green dress, the Queen sat upon her throne in the onyx hall. "Hello Quintus."

The bearded officer bowed. "Greetings. I congratulate your majesty on inspiring such an incredible victory."

"Thank you, but it was mainly down to our military men and women. They have done this realm proud. You, on the other hand, have not."

Quintus looked perplexed. "Pardon, your majesty? I am no soldier or commander."

"I know that, but do you not remember the advice you gave me? You convinced me that the Assyrian King would not invade. You told me to ignore him, which is exactly what I did, and look where it got us."

Quintus touched his chin. "Gosh. You are right. I gave your majesty my honest opinion. I genuinely surmised that h-"

"Well you surmised wrong! I won't be taking your advice again."

The Lord Treasurer nodded solemnly and looked down at Queen Ella's red shoes.

"Now then, we need to talk about matters of economy. Do we have the finances available to expand our armed forces?"

"Most certainly," Quintus said. "Our coffers have rarely looked healthier."

"How much can we increase our military allocation by?"

"I would say that we could double or perhaps even triple it."

Ella frowned. "I was hoping for rather more than that. We need a military that is capable of competing with the best."

"Well, invasions like this are very rare, so it may not necessarily be wise to keep a vast army. From what I understand, the Assyrian Empire will soon be a vassal of Praetoria, so they are unlikely t-"

The Queen put a hand up and the Lord Treasurer stopped talking. "I told you *not* to give me any more advice. If I listened to your ruinous logic, my realm would soon cease to exist!"

Quintus gulped. "You are right, most enlightened sovereign. I do apologise. I was just building up to a suggestion on how we could create a large army without spending much, but never mind."

"Why on earth would I want to hear any more of your suggestions? How many times do I have to say that I will not be following your advice ever again?"

"Your majesty would not have to follow it. I was merely throwing it out there."

There was silence for a while before Ella sighed. "Fine, just say it. You are clearly desperate to let it out. I could do with some entertainment to be honest. Your ideas always make me laugh."

Quintus cleared his throat. "Well, I was just talking to the Master of the Armoury, Sir Terin Cormin, and he said that they have collected a vast number of enemy swords and shields from the battlefield. These are items of good quality, and it occurred to me that perhaps we could give them to our people. We could create an auxiliary force composed of the loyal citizens of our beloved monarch. Those who are willing and able to fight could be called upon in times of need, by ringing the city bells for example. For a queen as popular as your majesty, there would be no shortage of volunteers. This auxiliary force could number in the region of ten thousand."

The Queen blinked her long eyelashes. "Auxiliary?"

"Ahem, yes, auxiliary. As in, an extra force, a reserve army if your majesty will, which would consist of non-professional soldiers."

Ella laughed. "Oh Quintus, that is the most terrible idea that I have ever heard! Firstly, why would I want to equip my people with weapons and armour which belonged to our enemy? Secondly, an army of citizens would be useless in battle. Thirdly, if I went round arming the commoners, they might decide to rise up against me. Then we would be in a real pickle. Once again, you have proved yourself to be a useless advisor!"

Dungeon Hark, who had been called earlier, entered the onyx hall. "Hello Dungeon. Thank you again for defending my realm so resolutely. I am eternally indebted and lucky that I have such a steadfast stalwart to rely on."

"It was an honour to serve our glorious queen," said the raven-haired commander. "It was also my duty and I will always defend this realm when it comes under attack."

Ella smiled. "In light of your deeds, I have decided to expand and improve your army. You and your soldiers demonstrated that you are every bit as competent as the Veraskans. With a bigger force under your command, I feel that you could be the true bulwark of Celtia."

"That is music to my ears."

"Of course, it will not happen overnight, because we must first replace the fallen. But that process seems to be going well, as our victory has inspired a new wave of recruits."

"Indeed, your majesty. Hundreds signed up at the barracks just this morning," Dungeon said.

"Excellent. So if I were to pledge to increase your regular soldiers to five thousand and your cavalry to eight hundred, would you be confident that such a force could keep my realm safe from any threat?"

"That would be an excellent improvement, your majesty. I am confident that such a force would be able to counter all but the greatest of threats."

"So you do not think that such a force could keep my realm safe from any threat?"

"Well, I cannot honestly make that guarantee. The Assyrians were able to bring eighteen thousand soldiers, so it is possible that others could bring more. However, with the Veraskans by our side, we would certainly be extremely formidable."

"I am not sure if I can count upon the Veraskans anymore," Ella said with a sigh. "They are not as courageous as I once thought."

Dungeon frowned slightly. "I was also surprised by some of their behaviour, but they were useful once they got going. They did not display the same level of bravery as my men though."

The Queen nodded. "Between you and me, I would replace Nina with someone more dependable if I could. But the Veraskans insist on choosing their own leader and I do not wish to disregard their traditions. They also lost half their numbers and replacing them will take a long time. I shall still utilise our elite force, but we ought to stop placing our faith in the myth of Veraskan invincibility."

"Wise words, your majesty. I certainly agree with your insight."

"I have an idea though," Ella said, "so tell me what you think. From the defeated Assyrians on the battlefield, we collected about ten thousand swords and shields. Suppose I were to create a reserve force, an *auxiliary* army, so to speak? We could give a sword and a shield to each person who is willing and capable of wielding them. In times of emergency, they could be called upon, by ringing the city bells for example. Hence, when required, you could have an additional ten thousand soldiers at your disposal." While the Queen spoke, she did not even glance at the Lord Treasurer.

Dungeon raised his brows. "That is a brilliant idea. Your majesty's genius is truly unparalleled. With such a large force, I am confident that we would be able to compete with the best."

Ella shrugged nonchalantly. "It was just an idea, and I had some doubts. You don't think that non-professional troops might be ineffective?"

"They would not be as effective or disciplined as our core regiments, but they would certainly be of use," Dungeon said. "There are many fit, strong, athletic people in our realm. There are farmers, hunters, labourers, merchants and the like who would all be capable of fighting. I am sure of it."

The Queen tilted her head. "Another concern I had was that it might be dangerous to arm peasants. What if they were to revolt?"

"In Celtia? Never. You are the most popular ruler that this realm has ever seen. You have done much for these people already. In their eyes, you can do no wrong."

"I thought so too," Ella said, "but I do not like to rely too much on my own opinions. Thank you for being so honest, Dungeon. I appreciate it."

"You're very welcome, and your majesty's prudence is admirable."

"I will put these plans swiftly into action. You may both leave now."

Queen Ella soon decided that she needed a break from the stresses of governing her realm. She thought about Viscount Elgar's invitation. His country estate sounded like the perfect getaway, so Ella put on a light yellow summer dress with white shoes, and got into a fast carriage with her bulldog.

They reached the nearby viscounty of Cosgrove in the afternoon, going down narrow country lanes bordered by wooden fences, mossy stone walls and tall hedges. As most of the land here was agricultural, they passed horses, cows and pigs in pleasant, hay-filled fields. After going through a picturesque red-and-white village, they turned off the road and entered a tree-lined avenue.

The main building of Elgar's country estate was an impressive limestone edifice, which various brick houses and beamed cottages surrounded. As the carriage pulled up on the gravel of the front garden, two little dogs scampered around the side of the mansion. A cocker spaniel and a cavalier spaniel barked at the visitors. Duncan seemed affronted and Ella had to prevent her pet from charging at the pretty dogs. But a brown mastiff came trotting along, and as the large canine loomed over Duncan, the bulldog's confident strut disappeared.

Three more dogs, a bloodhound, a wolfhound and a beagle, came scurrying. They were followed by the imposing, moustached figure of Viscount Elgar, who wore a cream suit and panama hat. His broad-shouldered frame limped along as he leaned on a gold-handled ebony cane.

"The royalty has arrived," declared the gent ebulliently as the ends of his grey moustache bounced. "Greetings your majesty," he said to Duncan and proceeded to shake the bulldog's paw, before turning to Ella. "Welcome to you too, miss."

The Queen smiled. "Hello Sir Elgar. How nice it is to be here today. What fine dogs you have."

Duncan froze shyly as the canine pack surrounded him, but then the bulldog leapt into action, bounding along the grass as the hounds playfully gave chase. Elgar chuckled at the whimsical sight. Four young women appeared from the mansion. "Indeed! What fine dogs I have!" The old man gestured to his daughters.

"Oh father," replied one of them. A dark-haired girl wearing an amaranth dress and a sunny smile stepped forward to greet the visiting monarch. "Hello your majesty. I am Emily." She curtsied. Miranda, Edith and Hannah introduced themselves equally cheerfully.

A mature lady in a white dress and flowery bonnet came out. "This is my beautiful wife Alice," said Elgar.

The lady smiled and suggested, "Perhaps her majesty would like a picnic?"

"That would be lovely," said Ella as sparrows spiralled above.

The viscount and the six women moved to the sprawling garden of the estate, in the middle of which stood a great oak. The sun shone as Lady Alice picked up a hamper and they made their way towards the stunning tree.

A tartan rug was placed on the ground in the shade of the oak's boughs. Bottles of apple juice from Elgar's orchard were poured into delicate china cups. Crab mayonnaise, cheese and pickle, and ham salad sandwiches were laid out, along with scones, strawberry jam and cream.

The women chatted about their dresses, shoes and hair, while Elgar wandered off to join the seven dogs frolicking in the field. The ladies watched as the gentleman would throw a stick and the hounds ran after it. But Elgar, who was a fast sprinter, would also give chase, and more often than not he ended up with the stick, thereby winning the game. He would then point his finger up and lecture the dogs on what they were doing wrong. Eventually, the canine company lost interest and excluded their master from playing with them.

The viscount returned to the girls. "Perhaps I could show her majesty my orchard?" Elgar was somewhat out of breath, his hair unkempt as he clutched his panama hat by his side.

"Certainly." Ella rose to her feet. "Thank you ever so much for the picnic, ladies." They gushingly returned her gratitude.

Elgar took Ella to the edge of the immaculately cut lawn and into the woods beyond. They entered an enormous orchard where apple trees extended for as far as the eye could see. The grey-haired gentleman hobbled along, leaning on his cane as he plucked an apple from a branch. He offered Ella the fruit, which she happily accepted despite having just drunk plenty of juice.

"Elgar, there is something that I have been meaning to talk to you about."

Munching on an apple, Elgar looked at Ella with those brown eyes which forever appeared somewhere between startled and bemused.

"Before my coronation, I went to visit the seer Saxophyllus," Ella said. "He gave me a prophecy and it has preoccupied me ever since."

The viscount continued to stare at the monarch. It was rare for Elgar to make long eye contact as his enigmatic gaze usually floated about. "What did the seer say?"

Ella took a deep breath. "He said that the one I seek for love possesses also a lock which matches my key." She reached into her pocket, pulled out her key and handed it to Elgar. He gazed upon the red porcelain rose, the smooth gold metal twisting around the green stem and the ridges of the key tip. "Saxophyllus also said that my one true love would invade my realm."

"And do you believe him?"

"Well, I had a feeling before I saw him that this key would lead me to my true love, so when he said it too..." Ella sighed and trailed off.

"Oh, I don't know. I suppose I am telling you this because you seem like such a wise and experienced man, Sir Elgar. I need advice because I sometimes feel like I am going mad."

Elgar nodded, curling his upper lip which made his thick moustache appear even more prominent. "Do not let his prophecy oppress you," the viscount offered earnestly. "Live your life full-bloodedly, and trust in yourself more than any other. If the prophecy happens, it happens. If it doesn't, it doesn't. Even a seer can be wrong." He handed the rose key back to Ella.

She nodded slowly and looked at a gently flowing brook on her left which shimmered in the sun. "Do you know anything about the Order of the Sacred Rose?"

The old man shook his head. "I have heard the name, but I know nothing about them."

"Well, I met a charming knight once, and he wore the emblem of the Order of the Sacred Rose. It looked very similar to my key. I really wish I had got to know him better."

Elgar shrugged. "I am sure that there are many fine young men, kings and emperors even, who would give anything to be yours."

"There are, and handsome ones too," Ella said. "But I always seem to end up pushing them away. I just don't know what I want, or who I want."

She tossed her apple core towards the river but Elgar caught it. "What are you doing?" he asked.

"Throwing my waste away."

"This is not waste." The viscount snapped the core in two and took out a small brown seed. "Do you know that one of these can grow into an apple tree?"

"Yes, of course, but there are thousands of apple trees in your orchard, Elgar. I'm sure that you don't really care about one seed."

"That's not my point."

"Then what is your point?"

"My point," Elgar said, "is that the seed is greater than the fruit."

Ella furrowed her brow in confusion. "I already know about seeds, Elgar. You need not educate me on botany."

"Then why do you fret over that handsome knight?"

Ella appeared irritated by the bizarre line of questioning. "What?"

"You are too concerned with form," Elgar stated. "Essence is more important than form."

"I really have no idea what you are talking about, Sir Elgar. If what you are getting at is that I care too much about looks, then I would point out that you put a lot of effort into your appearance. And your wife is very pretty too, so form is clearly important to you."

"Of course it is, but form without essence is nothing, whereas essence without form is something."

Ella's perplexed face was on the verge of a sullen scowl. "So what exactly are you trying to say?"

"That essence must always come before form."

"I see. And I suppose that you have both essence and form in abundance," the Queen remarked sarcastically.

"Exactly!" Elgar pointed a finger up. "But I acquired essence before I acquired form."

Ella's mouth hung open. "So you used to be ugly?"

"No, but I used to wear herringbone-patterned tweed."

The pair walked in silence for the rest of the time that they were in the orchard. Soon they were back on the large lawn and passed the great oak tree. "Can I show you my house?" asked Elgar.

"Of course. You know how much I like attractive things, Sir Elgar, and your house is no doubt both attractive and full of character."

The viscount grinned and led his royal guest into a glass conservatory at the back of the mansion. It was a humid and fragrant room full of beautiful and exotic plants. Elgar took Ella through an ivory door and into a vast sandstone hallway. He showed her teak bedrooms, silver bathrooms and grand lounges containing plush armchairs and opulent lampshades.

He then led her into a room which was entirely white. "What do you make of this room?"

Ella looked around the colourless chamber, which appeared empty and zestless to her. But she knew that if she said that, it would give Elgar the chance to philosophise and lecture her again, so she remarked, "What an exquisite room you have here."

Elgar's face contorted in puzzlement. "Exquisite?" he said, aghast. "It's hideous!"

"If you think that a completely white room is hideous, then why do you have one, Sir Elgar?"

"Because I haven't painted it yet."

CHAPTER 16 – HUNTED FLOWER

Days after visiting Elgar's country estate, Queen Ella had dinner with Quintus, Elgar, Gullivander, Dungeon and Nina in her castle. The main topic of conversation was Viscount Elgar's new mustard suede suit, or specifically how garish Nina found it. Duncan scurried around the wood-panelled dining hall to feed on scraps.

"Gully," said Ella, "when will you perform the rest of *The Lily of the Valley* for us? I am keen to know who the Queen Lily ends up with."

Gullivander looked at Duncan. "Is this one going to be around?"

"No. I am terribly sorry again that he ruined your play, but he also ruined my World Fayre." Ella sighed. "I no longer allow him anywhere there is even the slightest potential for catastrophe to occur."

Elgar spoke, "He has a nose for the grandiose, this one." The old man vigorously patted the bulldog who pawed at the edge of the table, able to smell the food above him but unable to see it. Elgar chuckled as Duncan tried to clamber onto a chair. It occurred to the others that there were certain similarities between the viscount and the bulldog. Both seemed to possess that same youthful excitability, boundless energy and quaint emotional vulgarity.

"I wrote a poem about him," Gullivander mentioned with a mouth full of greasy fowl.

"This bulldog brown and round,

To him it's all a game,

Boldly does he bound,

Disaster is his aim,

A carnival he downed,

Amid a farcical flame,

That troublesome hound,

King Duncan is his name."

The others clapped and the bard stuffed his face with potatoes and parsnips. "Anyway, *The Lily of the Valley* will be ready by the end of the week, your royal loveliness."

The Queen smiled. "Wonderful."

Ella asked her guests if they would like to join her on a hunt tomorrow. Elgar, being a country gentleman, was most enthused by the proposal, while Quintus was also keen. Dungeon and Nina, who had spent most of the evening flirting, decided that they were too busy with the tasks of rebuilding their armies. Gullivander opted out so that he could work on preparing his play. Those partaking in the hunt stayed in the castle for the night.

The following morning, Quintus and Elgar waited on their horses in the front courtyard. The Lord Treasurer wore hunting leathers with a crossbow attached to his back and a sword slung at his hip. The viscount sported the same mustard suit that he had worn the evening before, choosing to bring a longbow, a quiver full of arrows and a cutlass. The sun was bright and the two men were most excited about the hunt ahead.

Ella came out of her castle wearing a black dress and leather boots. As Duncan trotted along after her, Elgar glanced at the bulldog. "How many dogs are we bringing?"

"Just one," Ella said, patting Duncan.

Elgar appeared bewildered. "One? A hunt requires a pack of hounds to chase the foxes, your majesty. I know Duncan has a fine nose, but the little fellow will struggle on his own."

"Foxes? We won't be hunting any foxes." Ella looked at the bows and swords that the men were carrying. "You certainly won't be needing weapons, gentlemen."

Elgar's moustached face screwed. "What animals are we hunting that we do not need weapons?"

"We are not hunting animals," the Queen said in a chastising tone. "We are hunting flowers. I need to find a purple orchid to add to my garden. And your horses won't be much use either, because we'll mostly be in the woods, scouring the ground."

The two men glanced at each other and then got off their horses. Quintus suggested, "We might as well take some weapons, in case we come across bandits or beasts."

"What did I tell you about giving me advice?" Ella rolled her eyes. "We will be in the hills, so bandits won't be a problem, but bring whatever you want."

The men decided to drop their bows but kept their swords which would be useful for cutting through branches. Ella, Elgar, Quintus and Duncan departed the castle on foot, turning north shortly after leaving the front gate. It was a warm day and the group plucked blackberries as they descended through tranquil woods.

They reached a dry valley and started to ascend into wild hills, where Ella believed the elusive purple orchid lay. There was nothing much here except flowers and trees. The humid air was filled by the dull buzz of insects. Climbing a heathery slope, the four were soon high enough to see the grey and white spires of the Tundra Castle in the distance.

They entered a steep forest where they began to come across flora which they had never seen; huge ovate leaves, yellow lotus and lantern-shaped orange flowers. Ella picked some and placed them in her basket. Hearing dainty birdcalls which were also new to them, they stopped and fell silent as they listened to the peaceful sounds of the idyllic, slanting forest.

But their blissful moment was interrupted by an altogether less graceful noise. A periodic thudding came from further up the hill, getting slowly louder. The delicate flowers around the group started to tremble.

A large brown bear appeared from the bracken, stood up on its hind legs and roared. The four immediately scattered in all directions. The great beast charged at the beardy figure of Quintus Northwood. The Lord Treasurer drew his sword, but the bear swiped it out of his hand. Quintus stumbled down the meadow below the forest.

Ella and Duncan had scarpered swiftly, but Viscount Elgar turned and saw Quintus scrambling down the slope on hands and feet as he desperately sought to escape the rushing bear. The moustached maestro drew his cutlass. Though he knew that he could not win a duel against such a beast, he could not shirk this challenge when his friend was in peril. Elgar rushed nimbly down the hill as the sides of his mustard suit flapped about, managing to stay upright despite the steep incline.

The hulking bear caught Quintus's foot in his mouth and proceeded to shake him around like a ragdoll. Elgar was still some way behind, so he threw his sword, which spun through the air, and the blunt end struck the back of the furry menace. The animal bellowed, releasing the Lord Treasurer, who picked up a rock and hurled it at the face of his assailant. Elgar sprinted towards the bear, shouting and spreading his arms to make himself appear bigger.

It was enough to scare the beast, who lumbered away into nearby woods. Elgar picked up his cutlass and helped Quintus. Bleeding through a mangled leather shoe, the injured man leaned on the viscount. They ambled up the heathery slope and found Queen Ella crouching behind a boulder.

"Where is Duncan?" Ella exclaimed.

"He didn't go with you?" asked Elgar.

"No! He ran the other way."

Viscount Elgar looked at his friend's bleeding boot. "Well, Quintus will need to get back to the castle as soon as possible."

"I can't leave without Duncan," Ella cried.

"Don't worry about me," said Quintus. "I will hide here." He lay down in the thick shrubbery next to the boulder. "You go and locate the bulldog."

Elgar and Ella nodded. They rushed to the woods where the bear had first appeared. They scoured the thickets, glades and meadows along the hillside, but saw no sign of the stout fawn dog. After a quarter of an hour of searching, Elgar said, "One of us will have to take Quintus back."

A tear rolled down Ella's cheek. "Then I will stay here and find Duncan."

"No," said Elgar, "I won't let you. It is too dangerous."

They then heard the growls of two bears roaming further up the hill. The viscount pulled on the Queen's arm. "We'll have to return later with a bigger party. We will surely die if we remain."

They dashed away and returned to Quintus by the boulder. The wounded man got up and they made their way back to the Tundra Castle.

When there, Quintus was taken to the hospice. Ella and Elgar immediately organised a search party consisting of Veraskans. They hastily returned to the dry valley, heathery slope and bear-infested woods. They searched for Duncan through the day and night, but the boisterous bulldog was nowhere to be found.

When Queen Ella returned to her castle again, she collapsed on the floor and rested her head on the red cushion of Duncan's wicker basket. She cried her eyes out, eventually passing out from exhaustion.

Her only glimmer of hope was that they had seen no hints of a struggle between bulldog and bear. They had found no clues, no traces whatsoever, and Ella clung to the belief that the clever dog would eventually find his way home.

*

Gullivander was scheduled to perform his grand play, *The Lily of the*

Valley, in the onyx hall. Ella was scarcely in the mood for entertainment, but she thought it might allow her a brief respite from the distress.

The Queen sat on her throne and the curtains opened to reveal a wild setting similar to that displayed at the World Fayre. Those early scenes commenced which Ella had seen before. The cheerful coronation of Queen Lily was followed by the Poplar Prince's declaration of love, but the Lily berated him. The Wizard of the Willow appeared and cast an enchantment on the monarch, putting her in a slumber of the deep until her true love comes and wakes her.

Those humorous acts involving the Prince of the Pond, the Sun King and the Marvellous Master Magpie played out. But this time, only a flutter of paper birds were used rather than real ones. Ella remembered the debacle of the first performance. How she would like to see Duncan leap onto the stage and ruin this play again.

The sleeping Queen Lily would still not wake and the trio of potential suitors quarrelled. Then a figure appeared from the vines, dancing in a lithesome manner, wearing an ivy toga and a crown of leaves.

"I am the Emperor of the Ivy,
But you can call me Caesar,
I shall make the damsel lively,
For only I can please her,
I am that occidental star,
The deepest crimson wine,
I have travelled from afar,
To make the maiden mine."

The Sun King stepped forward, puffed his rotund chest out and protested.

"You are just a plant,
A poisonous one too,
Awaken her you shan't,
I am worthier than you,
I am that shining light,
That hot summer blaze,
So bow before my might,
Or burn beneath my rays."

The Emperor of the Ivy simply laughed at the Sun King and replied with a song of his own.

"Pompous shiny sphere,
Go ahead and hiss,
Your threats I do not fear,
I journeyed not for this,
The reason I came here,
Is to see the sleeping miss,
My dainty dame most dear,
I shall wake you with a kiss."

The Emperor of the Ivy smeared a leaf across his lips, leaned over the Queen Lily and planted a kiss. Suddenly she awoke. Ella gasped. The Lily rubbed her eyes and began to sing rather drearily.

"I was dreaming of a city,
By a sparkling crystal lake,
It really was so pretty,
A merry tune I'd make,
A most delightful ditty,
Oh for goodness sake,
What a frightful pity,
That now I am awake."

Suddenly she put a hand to her mouth.

"Oh my lips are laced!
I feel like I am stung,
A horrid thing I taste,
Venom on my tongue!"

The Prince of the Pond stepped forward to utter his condemnation.

"Now it is most clear,
The emperor is a fake,
Poison he did smear,
To make the lady wake."

The Marvellous Master Magpie also had his say on the matter, dancing around and flapping his wings.

"Villainy most vile,
This knave is no king,
Now listen to him howl,
As I strike him with my wing!"

The magpie spun towards the emperor, trying to hit him, but Caesar evaded and retorted.

"Slanderous and silly,

My love for her is true,
Pretty Queen Lily,
I am the one for you,
My empire is most great,
You know I am not wrong,
So now accept your fate,
To me you do belong."
The Queen Lily scowled and flailed her arms furiously.
"What absolute tripe,
Utter conceit and cheek,
You are not my type,
I would rather wed a leek,
Neither rich nor ripe,
Such arrogance you reek,
Haughty hysterical hype,
You are not the one I seek!"
The Emperor of the Ivy cut a dejected figure and slithered away through the thickets before turning.
"Now I am most forlorn,
A dilemma you have made,
My heart has just been torn,
But my love will never fade,
You pierce me like a thorn,
So now I leave this glade,
But because you show such scorn,
Your valley I shall invade!"
At that moment, a young messenger ran into the onyx hall. He stopped before the enthroned Queen Ella, who was visibly irritated that the performance had been interrupted.

"Your majesty, our realm is under attack! The Praetorian Empire marches eastward through the great plain!"

Ella blinked a few times. She looked at the messenger, then at the stage behind him, uncertain if this was real or part of the play. But as the Queen looked into the eyes of Gullivander and the actors, she realised that it was no thespian act.

"How many?" Ella asked in the faintest of voices.

"Three legions of five thousand soldiers each and five hundred cavalry."

Slumped in her seat, Ella gazed emptily at the stage before her. The

Queen Lily, the Sun King, the Prince of the Pond and the Marvellous Master Magpie stared at the monarch. There was a silence in the onyx hall which could have lasted for ten seconds or ten minutes; it was impossible to tell.

"Mobilise all my units at Fort Veraska," Queen Ella finally said to the junior messenger, and he ran off to inform senior staff.

"Would you like us to continue the play, your majesty?" Gullivander asked tentatively.

"Just tell me what happens at the end."

"The Queen Lily is on the cusp of defeat by the Emperor of the Ivy's legions, but the Poplar Prince comes to her rescue. They go off into the wilderness and live happily ever after."

Ella nodded slowly. Eventually she got off her throne and left the hall. She did not put on armour, remaining in a lilac dress, nor did she take weapons. The Queen mounted a horse and rode to Fort Veraska.

Surrounded by tall trees, the fort lay near the edge of the great plain. Sentries greeted the mounted monarch as spiked gates opened. On a large earthen square, Nina Veraska stood before a battalion of bronze-and-gold women.

"How many do you have?" asked Queen Ella.

"Six hundred infantry and one hundred and fifty cavalry."

The numbers seemed irrelevant, because Praetorians were allegedly invincible. All that they could do now was wait for Dungeon's army to arrive. Ella wandered around the fort complex, which consisted of numerous stone buildings within a metal perimeter. She thought about what it would be like to have been born a Veraskan, to be trained as a warrior from early infancy. These girls had no choice, no independence and no life beyond their duties of fighting and guarding. Ella weighed up the hard-but-simple existence of a Veraskan against the grand-but-complicated life of a monarch. She could not decide which seemed easier.

When Dungeon's forces arrived, they stayed in the woods outside Fort Veraska because there was not enough space inside. The raven-haired commander had brought four thousand regulars, eight thousand auxiliaries, one thousand archers and five hundred horse soldiers. Viscount Elgar would be the honorary cavalry commander, wearing the same moss green tweed suit which he wore to the last battle.

Ella felt a glimmer of hope for the first time. With an army of this size, at least they would not be vastly outnumbered. With good scouting and a superior knowledge of the lay of the land, the Queen hoped that her forces might somehow be able to out-manoeuvre or surprise the enemy.

When they reached the great plain, they received reports that the Praetorians were five miles to the west, meaning that they would probably clash in about an hour. Queen Ella convened her commanders and asked them to suggest tactics.

Nina Veraska answered first, "Our only possibility of victory is if we destroy the enemy cavalry with our archers. That way, we will be able to utilise our own cavalry to maximum effect. So hide archers in the woods, lure the enemy into a charge, and shoot. Of course, it's easier said than done, because Praetorians are tactically astute and they will be wary of getting too close to any woods. They will also have scouts themselves, and it will be difficult to hide unnoticed, but we don't have another option."

Dungeon nodded. "I do not disagree with the lady's logic. It seems sensible for my three regiments to engage their three legions head on. The enemy will eventually prevail, because they are Praetorians, but if we use our horses and archers to good effect then we might just have a chance."

Viscount Elgar concurred. Ella looked into the distance, where the charred remains of the World Fayre stood. The burnt canvas of large tents swayed in the wind. "Why don't we use those?" the Queen suggested. "I know it's not much, but the Praetorians will surely have the upper hand in the open field. That is the only real obstacle in this plain." She pointed at the debris. "If the enemy gets beyond it, then they have open field all the way to Livia."

Nina nodded. "It's true. We must make use of whatever small advantage we can find."

Dungeon and Elgar uttered their agreement, so the armies marched towards the carcass of the World Fayre. They passed through the area where the commoners had once celebrated. They saw the blackened remains of the palisade wall which had surrounded the designated section. Here, the elites of the world had gathered, including Gaius Romulus Caesar himself. Ella thought about the duel between the Praetorian Emperor and King Bosgald that day. Caesar had looked so superior, but the 'barbarian king' managed to ruffle his feathers.

The defenders of Celtia walked through flailing pieces of fabric and husks of wrecked tents. At the western perimeter, the wall was actually in reasonable condition; ten feet tall in parts which the fire had not reached.

"This is good," said Dungeon. "We can stretch our forces along this line. Then the enemy will not be able to outflank us. Let us have archers shooting over the walls and put the rest in the woods."

"Exactly what I was thinking," said Nina.

Dungeon's soldiers began to spread out in a line. In the south, where the wall was burnt to the ground, two of the three regiments were placed. One, an auxiliary regiment of four thousand armed citizens, stood with the woods on their left, while on their right was Dungeon's core regiment of four thousand professional soldiers. To the core's right was the palisade wall which stretched for half a mile, hugged by two hundred archers. On their right, Dungeon put his second auxiliary unit of four thousand, extending to the edge of the northern forest. Thus, there was one continuous line of troops across the width of the great plain.

Four hundred archers went into the woods on the north side and the same number went to the south. They moved slightly west so that they would be able to shoot out into the open plain as the enemy approached.

Now that they had a solid defence sorted, the commanders could start thinking about how to utilise their most potent attacking weapons, Elgar's cavalry and the Veraskans. Dungeon suggested perhaps luring one Praetorian legion beyond the defensive line and cavalry-charging them there.

Nina disagreed. "If the Praetorians do not fall for it, then our best offensive units are stifled back here. Cavalry would be ineffective in such a cramped space anyway. Just stick them in the woods. Let us not make this too complicated. The enemy is trying to conquer us, so the onus is on them to attack. We should have the element of surprise on our side and we can wait for the perfect moment to strike."

The raven-haired commander nodded and the moustached viscount was also happy with the plan. The Veraskans went into the southern forest, closer to the defensive line than the archers, and Elgar's cavalry went into the northern forest.

Queen Ella stood alongside Dungeon Hark behind their defences. In the great plain, the clouds could be seen for many miles and their vastness could be truly appreciated. The apparent infiniteness of the land and the sky added to a portentous aura, as an epic battle was about to begin, which felt like the colossal end-of-world clash depicted in so many myths and folklore.

CHAPTER 17 – THE HIDDEN FLAME

Caesar's legions appeared on the horizon, shimmering like mirages under the sun. A long line of silvery metal streaked with red marched ominously towards the defenders of Celtia. Dungeon's soldiers murmured amongst themselves as they gazed towards those apparently invincible conquerors of the Earth. But the raven-haired commander reminded his troops that, although the enemy looked celestial, Praetorians were indeed humans.

Queen Ella felt queasy. To take her mind off the situation, she glanced around at the remains of that jovial midsummer carnival, the World Fayre. Ella recognised the burnt shell of her vast tent which had once been a paradisiacal purple pavilion. Parts of it still stood, the loose canvas waving around in a gentle breeze. Ella saw a small opening and scrambled through a collapsed corridor. She found herself in a tiny chamber with no space to stand. A sheet of burgundy silk, seemingly untouched by the fire, hung from the low ceiling.

Ella lay on the ground, imagining that she was camping in a little tent in the meadows. Her rose key fell out of her pocket, so she picked it up and ran her fingers over those red porcelain petals and the smooth metal which twisted around the stem. A breeze coursed through the chamber, causing the sheet above Ella to sway, and a piece of paper fluttered over the Queen. She caught it and saw a poem written in gold ink.

"In the darkness of the depths below,
Where no light had ever been,
A candle lit and seemed to glow,
As bright as day although unseen,
There does that tender secret dwell,
Forever since the day you came,
To you alone my heart does swell,
For you invoked the hidden flame."

Ella stared at the letter. Feeling unnerved, she scrambled out of the tent, and looked around but saw nobody nearby. She was unsure if the wind had brought the note into the tent or if it had already been in there. Ella moved away from the eerie ruins and returned to Dungeon behind his defensive line.

The enemy was now near. The sound of their stomping was as

impressive as the appearance of their armour. The three legions stepped in perfect sync as the rhythm of their strides made the ground shake. The fabled soldiers held up their rectangular shields and gripped their *gladius* swords by their sides, while behind them loomed the Praetorian cavalry.

Parts of the legions broke off and went into the forests at their edges. They seemed to know that archers were hidden there and dealt with them efficiently and effortlessly. Ella and Dungeon watched as their ranged units were led out of the woods, bound and captive, and taken beyond enemy lines. The Celtian archers would not get the opportunity to carry out their surprise attack. Praetorians were far too clever to fall for such a simple ploy. The Veraskans and Elgar's cavalry were also hidden in the forests but they saw what was coming and withdrew to deeper woods.

The legions marched steadily towards the line of green-and-purple infantry. They halted and a wave of rocks flew through the air above, launched by ballista behind.

The hail of boulders crumpled shields and threw Celtian soldiers back. Dungeon's regiments would be decimated if this continued. Their morale was already seen to be wavering, so the raven-haired commander was left with no choice but to blow his war horn.

A thunder filled the plain as the defenders roared their battle cries and charged at the invaders. Bronze struck iron along a front which stretched from forest to forest.

The enemy cavalry and archers simply waited behind their legions, which made it impossible for Elgar's cavalry to charge, but the restless viscount could not stand still. He saw the infantry attack infantry head-on, so his cavalry would attack cavalry head-on. If they did it quickly enough, the Praetorian archers would be unable to shoot for fear of hitting their own horses.

The moustached maestro raised his sabre and five hundred horses galloped through the thickets. Emerging from the woods in the shape of an arrowhead, they were swiftly upon the exposed flank of the Praetorian cavalry. Enemy horsemen frantically turned to face this unforeseen threat but Elgar's sharp offensive penetrated the unit. The green-and-purple horsemen slashed furiously at their red-crested opponents, who suddenly did not seem so invincible.

Viscount Elgar quickly realised that his force held the advantage here, since they had wiped out the centre of the Praetorian cavalry.

While the enemy had a loose circle around them, his own unit had a compact formation, which could be exploited by bursting outwards. He gave the command and the Praetorian horsemen were soon scattering in every direction.

For all their military academies and tactical training, the Praetorians had been startled by Elgar's bold offensive manoeuvring. Ella and Dungeon felt lifted when they saw it. The enemy was not flawless after all, and while their cavalry was dispersed, Elgar perceived a further opportunity. Ahead of his cavalry were the Praetorian archers, who were notching their arrows, so the mounted soldiers charged and rapidly destroyed the unit. Both sides were now robbed of their archers and it would be a battle of only infantry and cavalry.

In the main engagement, Caesar's army had barely been dented by Dungeon's infantry. That line of iron tower shields was virtually impenetrable and the legionaries were very efficient in the thrusting of their swords. Dungeon's two auxiliary forces were thinning fast and his core regiment of professional soldiers was faring only slightly better. The Veraskans, still in the woods, would have to alleviate the pressure on Dungeon's troops by attacking the Praetorian rear.

But the enemy cavalry was regrouping in the distance. About three hundred of them remained while Elgar had four hundred. The offensive viscount shouted and a tide of green-and-purple surged down the great plain. Though the Praetorian cavalry were outnumbered, they could not be seen to lose face again, and met Elgar's onrushing horsemen head-on.

The Veraskans got the hint and charged from the southern forest. First, a line of horsewomen rained down upon the rear of the legions. Then the Veraskan infantry laid siege to those parts which had already been softened. Many Praetorians fell as the exposed legionaries were too slow to get into defensive shape.

The two cavalry hordes played out their faraway battle which had become chaotic after the initial straightforward collision. There were no real tactics in this frenzied mounted melee but the greater number of Elgar's force began to tell. Some junior Praetorians fled westward while the rest fought to the last horse, because the word 'surrender' did not exist in their lexicon.

By the end of the bloody encounter, the entire Praetorian cavalry regiment had been vanquished. Brimming with confidence, Elgar's seventy horsemen cantered across the plain to assist their comrades.

The Veraskan cavalry had enjoyed considerable success with their rear charges, cutting down a few hundred legionaries while losing only a few dozen of their horsewomen.

But Praetorians were fast learners and they organised their entire back line into a tight turtle formation. From forest to forest stretched a wall and ceiling of tower shields. Not a chink existed for Elgar to exploit. The dogged viscount nonetheless tried, but for the first time his charges were impotent. The Veraskan infantry also struggled to make further impact.

The situation was much grimmer for Dungeon's forces. His two auxiliary regiments were being cut to pieces and the volunteers were fast losing stomach to fight such superbly skilled opponents. The farmers, hunters, labourers and tradesfolk of Celtia were exhausted and exasperated by an increasingly hopeless state of affairs.

Suddenly, the northern auxiliary unit routed, starting as a trickle and quickly becoming a river of people fleeing into nearby woods. A section of the legion which had faced them broke off and hastily rounded up groups of the distressed citizen-soldiers. The rest of that legion speedily moved forward and swung round to assault the right flank of Dungeon's core regiment. Of the four thousand professional soldiers which Dungeon had started with, about half remained, and that number looked set to plummet further.

Then the other auxiliary unit gave up all hope and routed into the southern woods, where they too were pursued by Praetorians. The rest of the unoccupied legion swung round to assail the left flank of Dungeon's main force.

The encounter now appeared to be as good as over. Celtia still had some Veraskans, but the Praetorians were fighting with all the efficiency, tactical discipline and invincibility for which they were famed. Ten thousand legionaries enveloped Dungeon's last standing soldiers.

The raven-haired commander waved a white flag. "We surrender. This battle is finished." Dungeon did not want to see his men needlessly slaughtered. Nina Veraska's women threw down their axes and Elgar's cavalry simply watched from afar. There was nothing else that they could do now. Some of the horsemen rode away because they did not wish to become slaves of the Praetorian Empire.

Queen Ella watched in horror from behind the palisade wall. She was angry and upset that her forces had given up but she also recognised the inevitability of their defeat. The Praetorians were simply too good at what they did. Celtia had effectively been conquered and Ella now had two choices. She could either flee and never return, or face the scarlet emperor who had invaded her realm.

As Ella saw Dungeon's men being bound and separated, she felt a pang of guilt. After all that her forces had given, she could not run away. Ella rode on her grey horse towards the swathe of crimson conquerors, her lilac dress fluttering as she sought to locate Gaius Romulus Caesar.

The red sea parted and a man walked forward. On his shining chest plate was the golden imprint of an eagle's wings. Tasselled plates adorned his shoulders, puffy sleeves covered his arms and a crested helmet rested on his head. On his back, a scarlet cape billowed.

The legionary moved towards Queen Ella, who dismounted her horse. Her body trembled and her big blue eyes gaped. Caesar removed his helmet and the untamed curls of his dark hair bounced free. His amber eyes seemed to be filled with a sort of maniacal exhilaration; a particular euphoria which perhaps only the ruler of an all-conquering empire could experience.

"Queen Lily." A tear rolled down Ella's cheek as her golden-brown hair waved in the wind. "This beautiful realm is now a province of my empire. I shall rename it *Lilium*," said Caesar. "I may be the rose of the world, but you are the lily of my valley. Do you now accept your fate?"

Ella stared at the grass. Just as Caesar opened his mouth to speak again, a thunderous sound reverberated through the plain and the earth trembled.

The emperor turned to see that an enormous boulder had landed in the middle of his second legion. Men were screaming as injured Praetorians crawled along the ground. Caesar's scarlet cape rippled behind him as he analysed the unbelievable scene, seeming unable to come to terms with what had just happened.

Then another great rock eclipsed the sun as it flew through the sky, and wiped out more legionaries. A third one struck the ground, tearing up turf. The boulders were coming from the northern woods, so a Praetorian captain ordered his men to pour forward.

Suddenly, a huge line of warriors appeared from the forest. They wore animal skins and fur capes, held colossal axes, and shouted savagely as they charged at the legions.

"Barbarians," Caesar murmured. "Engage them!" He grabbed Ella by her elbow.

The swarm of long-haired fighters enveloped the Praetorian Third Legion, which had no time to get into formation. Caesar called his unit of bodyguards and they followed him as he pulled Queen Ella towards the southern woods.

The scarlet emperor stopped when they were on the forest edge. Ella screamed as she saw a boulder hurtling at them. Caesar turned his head just as it landed. The rock wiped out his bodyguard and flung him forward.

Suddenly, Caesar was on top of Ella, who shrieked and flailed her arms. "Get off me!"

But when Ella looked into Caesar's amber eyes, they appeared glazed and distant. His mouth opened but his speech slurred, "I-I c-can't…"

Ella squirmed, wrestling the armoured emperor, and managed to struggle free from under him. She got up and saw that Caesar's cape was torn, his right arm was badly twisted and there was a gaping wound in his right leg.

"J-Jupitus, M-Marconius, aid me!" Caesar shouted from the ground, but when he turned his neck, he saw that they were dead. The scarlet emperor looked up at Ella. For the first time, she recognised a powerlessness in his eyes. Extending a shaking arm, he pleaded, "H-Help me."

Ella's caring gaze regarded the weak and wounded man. She kneeled and pulled him into a sitting position. Caesar gestured to the woods so Ella helped to move him there. The injured emperor pointed at a large tree covered in ivy, which Ella guided him to. Caesar leaned against the thick trunk, his breathing laboured and skin pale. Then he closed his eyes and slumped to the ground.

The queen's tears splashed onto the emperor's sculpted face as he lay among the ivy. She took his scarlet cape and placed it over his body. While the ferocious tempest of battle flared outside the forest, Ella sat down with the withering Emperor of the Earth. She held his hand and closed her eyes.

Ella may have been unconscious for one minute or one hour, but the moment that she opened her eyes, she saw a flash of brown fur on the edge of the woods. She rose to her feet. "Duncan!" Ella screamed in delirium and began to run. She manically sprinted up a slope to pursue what was most likely just a deer or hare.

Ella was on the verge of collapsing when she reached the top of the knoll but she kept going. She entered a wheat field as grains swirled around the air, clinging to her dress and hair.

Ella stopped and found herself in a small clearing. All around, golden crops swayed in a breeze as the tops of mature wheat glistened under the sun. A bare, hollow tree protruded from the cracked earth. From its boughs hung a huge cream sail.

As a strong wind coursed through the field, many pieces of canvas cloth fluttered about. Suddenly Ella recognised them as the sails of Ronwind Drake's airship, which had launched from the World Fayre. That day, the little adventurer had departed for the clouds. This was how far he had gotten. This wheat field near the great plain was where Ronwind's ambitious voyage had ended. Here, his monumental contraption had crashed, and the plucky pioneer was probably dead.

As Ella looked around at the fabric swaying among the glittering sea of grain, she realised that she stood in a field of cloth and gold. Then she heard the galloping of hooves. Coming straight at her was a robust, bearded figure riding a dark horse. An auburn cape flowed behind him and he was flanked by two other horsemen.

"Queen Ella! It is I, King Bosgald of Borra. My army has shattered those legions which invaded your realm." Four men appeared behind him, carrying a huge golden chest like a holy ark. "I am the one you seek and I know of the prophecy concerning your key."

The chest was brought before Ella, dust spiralling as it was placed on the ground. The shining object was garnished with gems of many colours and on its front hung a large lock. "Together we will forge an everlasting dynasty," King Bosgald declared. "We shall rule the world between us. This chest possesses tremendous treasures and you will find that its lock is that which matches your key."

Ella stood in a silent stupor, swaying like wheat in the wind. With a trembling hand, she reached into her pocket and pulled out her rose key. She ran her fingers along the gold metal which twisted around the stem, and grasped the porcelain flower.

She stepped forward and placed the tip of the key into the lock. It seemed to fit, and turned, but no click came, as the key simply rattled. She tried a second time, but again the mechanism failed to activate.

"Give me that," Bosgald barked. He took Ella's key and plunged it into the lock. Again, it just jangled, like any key would which was too small for the hole. The barbarian king tried pushing it in at different angles, but nothing happened. One of his men tried. "This key is the wrong size, your majesty."

King Bosgald flew into a fit of rage and glowered at Ella, who quivered. The bearded monarch threw the rose key to the earth and it landed just before Ella's feet.

Suddenly a horn blared in the distance and Bosgald turned to view the valley that the wheat field overlooked. On the far side, an armoured column moved down through fog and then disappeared into a belt of woodland.

"Curse Praetoria!" Bosgald exclaimed. "They never know when to give up!" He turned to one of his horsemen. "Go and ensure that my men are prepared. Wait. In fact, have them form a line at the edge of this field, so that we can descend upon the enemy in the valley."

The aide galloped off to deliver the message. After their violent and hard-fought victory over the Praetorians, only a few hundred of King Bosgald's troops remained. They trudged up the slope and assembled on the grassy plateau beneath the field of cloth and gold.

The barbarians gripped their weapons and waited for the enemy to appear at the foot of the valley, but a quarter of an hour passed and nothing came. "Where are they?" Bosgald demanded.

"Must still be in the woods on the other side of the vale," said a red-haired warrior.

Suddenly, a flurry of silver appeared on the right of the horde. They then realised that what they thought had been the silver of Praetorian armour was in fact the silvery grey of fur.

Hundreds of wolves, faster than men, rushed towards the barbarians and snarled, snapping their jaws and lunging. They rapidly engulfed the right side of the formation and dragged soldiers to the ground.

"Bring men from the left!" Bosgald bellowed. Those troops on the left turned, but as they did, a burst of brown fur emerged behind them. Dozens of hulking bears charged towards their backs, clawing, gnawing and flinging terrified warriors around.

King Bosgald watched dumbfoundedly from above as a legion of wolves and bears tore his army to shreds. He turned to Ella. "What queen are you who commands the animal kingdom? Who grants you such power?" He pointed his sword. "Thou must be a witch!"

But Ella was observing the scenes with the same level of amazement. Then a shaggy figure surged through the wheat, and in a flash, dragged one of the king's aides into the crops.

Shortly thereafter, a spear flew through the air and struck the other horseman, who slumped to the ground. Now Bosgald had no protection, so he drew his sword and shield. "Show yourself!"

A man with flowing brown hair appeared from the wheat. Quick as a wolf, he dashed in front of King Bosgald's steed. The startled horse bucked and the heavy monarch tumbled to the earth. He scrambled to his feet as the man with the spear rushed towards him, putting his shield up just in time to block the weapon, which snapped in two.

The barbarian king went on the offensive, swinging his sword like a madman, but his assailant was too fast. The mysterious man seemed to be playing games as he effortlessly dodged Bosgald's blade. As Ella watched, it reminded her of the scene at the World Fayre when King Bosgald had faced Gaius Romulus Caesar.

Suddenly, a horse bolted between the duelling pair and the athletic figure was knocked to the ground. Dazed by the impact, he looked up with startled eyes, seeming vulnerable for the first time. Bosgald charged with his great sword held high, but just as he was about to reach the defenceless man, he felt a powerful force pull him back. He fell on his front and the weapon flew from his hand.

He turned his head to see a stout fawn dog clamped onto his boot, the grip of his large jaw vice-like. Pressing his flat snout against the king's ankle, the bulldog clung on with all the tenacity and stubbornness for which the breed was famed. Duncan growled and shook Bosgald's foot from side to side as though he had just caught a rabbit.

The mysterious figure appeared above the fallen monarch. "Tarva, Leino." Some wolves appeared and Bosgald was dragged into the carnage below.

As the man looked at Ella, she realised who he was. He had piercing blue eyes and a scar on both cheeks. He wore tanned leather to his knees, beneath which were his powerful calves. Ella stared at the vagabond with wide eyes.

"I am the one for you. We met a long time ago, in the woods, and I fell in love."

"B-But, the seer," Ella murmured. "H-he said..."

"What did he say?"

"He said that my one true love would carry a lock matching my key, and that it would guard a chest carrying tremendous treasures. He would bring an everlasting dynasty and come to conquer my realm."

"Then he was not wrong," the vagabond said and pulled an object from his breast pocket. It was a red rose, around which was wrapped a lock of golden hair. "I do indeed carry a lock, and it is your lock, which my wolf tore that fateful night. Ever since, it has guarded my chest, within which you will find the treasure of my heart."

"Our love is an everlasting dynasty," he declared. "And answer me this. Have I not conquered your realm already?"

Ella fainted in the field of cloth and gold, for she knew that he was the one. The vagabond picked her up and carried her home.

As the sun set, a bard watched from a distant hill and strummed on his lute.

"In a golden field lay a locked chest,
As our fairy tale comes to a close,
A melodramatic love quest,
In which empires came to blows,
Many declared they were the best,
But only one the Queen Lily chose,
For he had risen above the rest,
To win the heart of the world rose."

Thus, on the day that the world rose, there was one who had won *The World Rose*.

Made in the USA
Charleston, SC
28 March 2015